WILD BULL

Clint stood up and walked to Hanson's table, with D. L. Bonney right behind him . . .

Hanson gave them both a long look, then put his beer mug down and narrowed his eyes. Clint assumed that the narrowing of the eyes was supposed to scare him. "I don't remember invitin' you gents to set down."

"You're Hanson, aren't you?" Clint asked.

"That's right, stranger," Hanson said. "You recognized me, huh?"

"No," Clint said, "not you, just the ludicrous get-up."

"Are you sayin' I look silly?" he demanded of Clint.

"I'm sorry," Clint said. "Didn't I speak English? You . . . look . . . ridiculous!"

"Do you know who you're talkin' to?" Hanson asked.

"I'm talking to a silly ass who thinks he's a Hickok look-alike."

THE GUNSMITH

178
WILD BULL

J. R. ROBERTS

JOVE BOOKS, NEW YORK

WILD BULL

A Jove Book / published by arrangement with
the author

PRINTING HISTORY
Jove edition / October 1996

The Putnam Berkley World Wide Web site address is
http://www.berkley.com/berkley

ISBN: 0-515-11957-1

A JOVE BOOK®
Jove Books are published by The Berkley Publishing Group,
200 Madison Avenue, New York, New York 10016.
JOVE and the "J" design are trademarks
belonging to Jove Publications, Inc.

PRINTED IN THE UNITED STATES OF AMERICA

10 9 8 7 6 5 4 3 2 1

THE GUNSMITH

178

WILD BULL

ONE

They were facing each other on the main street of a town called Springfield, Missouri. On both sides of the street people were lined up to watch the action. One man in particular was interested. His name was D. L. Bonney, and he was a writer.

Bonney was watching the action intently, although—at the moment—there wasn't much action going on. The two men were just staring at each other.

Actually, one of them was a man and the other little more than a boy. He was wearing a gun, though, and in the eyes of most people who lived in the West—and some who lived in the East—a gun made a man out of a boy pretty quickly.

The two figures stood fifty feet apart. Bonney was perhaps that far from the older man, but close enough to the younger to see him bite his lower lip and worry it a bit.

A bad sign. If he was nervous about what he was doing,

why had he pushed it so? He had given the older man virtually no choice in the matter. If he had not stepped out into the street to face him, he would have been branded a coward. As such, he would have become the target of many even more cowardly gunmen seeking to make a name for themselves. Perhaps even more of a target than he already was.

Bonney had his notebook out and was busily writing what he saw. He wrote about the people who were watching, about how hungry the looks on their faces were. They were waiting anxiously for both men to draw their weapons, and for someone to die. This was some excitement in the middle of their boring lives, and they were hanging on every moment, every movement, every breath the two men took.

Bonney was fascinated by whatever it was that made men—and women, and some children, too—eagerly await bloodshed and death.

In point of fact, D. L. Bonney was in Springfield for an entirely different reason. He was looking for a man, and neither of these two was him. He had walked into the middle of this situation and, as a newspaperman, *had* to stop and watch and record what he saw.

He had arrived in Springfield three days before and, having traveled from the East, had particular hungers when he arrived. The first had been a meal, the second a drink, and the third a woman. He had enjoyed the three so well that he continued to indulge in all of them each day, while waiting for his man to arrive.

That morning and afternoon he had been in bed with his favorite whore, Candy. She was a buxom blonde in her early twenties who had been impressed when he told her he was a newspaperman.

"How long are you gonna keep waitin' for this fella to get here, honey?" she'd asked that morning.

"Not much longer, Candy," he'd answered, looking down at her. She had been positioned between his legs, playing with his penis until it lifted and hardened and was just about poking her in the nose.

Now she grasped it between her thumb, forefinger, and middle finger and stroked it up and down.

"Are you gonna forget me when you leave?"

"Uhh," he groaned, then said, "no way that's gonna happen, darlin'."

"Well," she said, licking her lips and opening her mouth, "we'll just see that it stays that way."

Bonney's legs were weak while he dressed. Candy was quite expert at everything she did. She had sucked him so effectively that he felt as dry as the desert. If she approached him again he was sure that he would not be able to rise to the occasion—not for an hour or so, at least.

While dressing he had walked to the window and peered outside. That's when he saw the commotion on the street.

"What's going on down there?"

Candy padded naked to the window and pressed up against him so she could see outside. His penis reacted to her presence and made a liar out of him. He wouldn't have needed an hour at all.

"Oh, it's a gunfight," she said.

"What?"

"Ain't you ever heard of—"

"Of course I've heard of it," he said. "I've just never seen one before."

"Well, it's goin' on now, darlin'."

"Shit," he said. "I better get down there and cover it."

"Cover it?"

"For my newspaper."

He pulled his boots on and grabbed his notebook and headed for the door.

"Honey," she called after him, "are you comin' back . . . ?"

But he was already gone.

So he, at least, had a reason for standing on the sidelines, waiting for something to happen. No such excuse existed for the others.

Up to this point most of Bonney's work had been done in the East. This was his first trip west, and so it was his first gunfight. He watched in fascination as the older man tried to talk the younger out of it. Was he that confident— or was he afraid?

"We don't have to do this, son," the man said.

"I have to do it," the younger man answered, "and don't call me son, old man."

Well, the older man wasn't *that* much older that he should be called "old man."

"I'm just giving you a chance to walk away clean," the man said. "Nobody here will think any less of you for coming to your senses."

"G'wan," a man's voice called out from the sidelines, "draw, awready."

"See?" the younger man said, with a sweep of his left arm—he was right-handed, and kept his gun hand at his side. "Even they demand it."

"Don't let one idiot talk you into dying," the older man said. "When this is over he'll walk away, and you won't."

The young man sneered and said, "So you say."

"Look—"

"We've done enough talking, old man," the young man said. "Let's do it."

"Don't—" the other man shouted, but it was too late.

Bonney watched in disbelief as the young man cleared leather first because the other man let him. Still, it was the other man who brought his gun up and fired first.

D. L. Bonney had never imagined that you could hear a bullet strike a man, but he did. He heard the bullet strike the young man in the chest, and saw the blood spurt forth and splatter in the dirt scant seconds before the man fell facedown in it.

The older man walked over to the fallen young one, knelt and examined him, then stood and holstered his gun. A man wearing a badge stepped into the street and approached the two, but as the older man turned to walk away the lawman hesitated and took a step back, either from respect or fear.

No one moved until the victor had left the field of battle, and then suddenly everyone was moving.

Bonney stepped into the street and walked over to where the dead man was lying. The sheriff reached the body when he did.

"Sheriff, my name's D. L. Bonney."

"Good for you." The sheriff was a hard-faced man in his forties, his face even harder while he stared down at the dead man.

"I'm a newspaperman. Can you tell me what happened here?"

The sheriff looked at him as if he were crazy.

"Weren't you here for the whole thing?" he asked. "A man was shot to death."

"But what about the other man?"

"What about him?"

"You just . . . let him go."

The sheriff averted his eyes.

"It was a fair fight," he mumbled.

"The other man was much faster."

"The kid pushed it," the lawman said. "He was askin' for it."

"You seem to have a lot of . . . respect for this other man," Bonney said. And fear, he added to himself. "Why is that?"

"Don't you know who he is?"

Bonney shook his head.

"No, I don't know who he is."

"Mister," the sheriff said, "that was Clint Adams . . . you know, the Gunsmith?"

"Oh," Bonney said, "the Gunsmith."

He felt disappointed.

"You know who the Gunsmith is, don't you?" the sheriff asked.

"I do," Bonney said. "But who doesn't? I was hoping it was somebody else."

TWO

Clint entered the saloon, feeling angry. He always felt angry when some damn fool forced him to kill him—especially when that fool was some kid who hadn't lived even a fraction of his life yet. He'd been in Springfield, Missouri, for two days, just relaxing. Today was to be his last day there, but he hadn't been able to get away before trouble started.

He marched to the bar and ordered a whiskey from the bartender, who had just barely beaten him back from the street. He rarely drank whiskey, so he tossed it back quickly and then asked for a beer.

"It weren't your fault, Mr. Adams."

Clint grabbed his beer, splashing some of it on the bar.

"I know," he said bitterly. "It never is."

"Are you going to talk to Adams, Sheriff?" Bonney asked.

7

"That's my job."

"When?"

The man scowled.

"As soon as I get this mess cleaned up."

With that he turned and called out for three men to come and pick up the dead man and take him to the undertaker's.

"What was his name?" Bonney asked, indicating the dead man.

"Damned if I know."

"He wasn't from here?"

"Naw," the lawman said. "He just rode in today."

"And Adams?"

"He ain't from here."

"When did he get to town?"

"Two days ago," the sheriff said. "Just passin' through, he said—but he stayed long enough to attract trouble, didn't he?"

"Are you saying this was his fault?"

"I'm sayin'," the man answered, "that if he sets and lights long enough, trouble catches up to him, just like it did today."

"And what do you intend to do about it?"

The sheriff looked at Bonney and said, "Well, I guess I'll be askin' him to leave town, won't I?"

"Will you?"

The man continued to scowl and didn't answer. Obviously the man didn't relish the task.

"Sheriff," Bonney said, brandishing his notebook, "how do you spell your name?"

Clint took his beer to a back table and sat there while some of the people filed back into the saloon. He'd been sitting there when the young man had first entered and started badgering him. He'd resisted as long as he could, but there were just too many people in the saloon. If he'd gotten up and walked away, word would certainly have gotten around. Besides, the young man never would have let him walk away. He had that look in his eyes, the look Clint had seen many times before. One way or another one of them was going to end up dead, and Clint was determined that it was not going to be him.

No matter what happened, he was always determined that it wouldn't be him.

D. L. Bonney followed the sheriff to the saloon, having given the man false courage by asking for his name and the correct spelling. Now the man was sure he was going to be written up in the newspapers as the man who chased Clint Adams out of his town.

Now all that remained was to see if he could actually do it.

THREE

Clint saw the sheriff enter the saloon and knew what was coming. It was always the way. If they didn't want him out of their town as soon as he rode in, they wanted him out after the trouble. Why? The trouble was over, wasn't it? How often did lightning strike in the same place?

Still, he never fought them. If the sheriff wanted him to leave, he'd leave. The town held bad memories for him, anyway, and nothing else.

"Adams?"

Clint looked up from his beer and into the man's eyes. He thought he saw the sheriff take a mental step backward. He couldn't take a physical step back because there was another man behind him, holding a notebook in his hands.

"Sheriff."

"Bumbry," the man reminded him, "Horace Bumbry."

"I remember." Clint had a feeling that the man had not said his name for his benefit. He suddenly realized that the man behind him must be a newspaperman.

"What can I do for you, Sheriff?"

"I think you know."

"The kid pushed it," Clint said. "I've got plenty of witnesses."

"There's no question about that," Bumbry said.

"You just want me to leave, right?"

That seemed to throw the man off balance. He had probably wanted to *tell* Clint to leave in front of the newspaperman. He hadn't expected Clint to suggest it, himself.

"I think you better leave my town," Bumbry said, "before there's more trouble."

"I'll finish my beer first, if you don't mind?"

"Uh . . . and then you'll leave?"

Clint nodded.

"And then I'll leave. There's nothing to keep me here anyway."

"I, uh . . ."

"Too easy for you, Sheriff? Did you think I'd fight to stay in your town?"

"I, uh . . ."

Clint looked past Bumbry and said to the man with the notebook, "We haven't met. I'm Clint Adams."

"I know who you are, Mr. Adams," the man said. He was younger than both Clint and the sheriff by ten years or so, maybe more. "My name is D. L. Bonney."

The man paused, as if Clint might know the name. He didn't.

"I'm a writer."

"A newspaperman?"

"Yes," Bonney said, "but essentially, I'm a writer."

"Oh? And did you see something you think you might write about today?"

"Well, I thought I had," Bonney said, "until I learned that you were involved."

"Why did that change your mind?"

"May I sit down?"

"Unless the sheriff insists that I leave town now."

Both men looked at the sheriff, who stammered that there was no hurry, as long as he left today, and then left the saloon.

"I think you embarrassed him," Bonney said, taking a seat at the table.

"Did he think you were going to write about him?"

"I suppose he did."

"But he didn't get that idea from you, right?"

Bonney smiled.

"Well, maybe he did."

"So tell me, Mr. Bonney, why you have no interest in writing about me."

"Does that upset or offend you?"

"No," Clint said, "on the contrary, it's a welcome change. I am, however, curious about why the change has come about."

"Well," Bonney said, "to be brutally truthful, you've been written about quite a bit over the years."

"That is the truth, but not brutally so."

"Well, here comes the brutal part."

"I'll try to bear up."

"People aren't that interested in you anymore."

"Because I've been written about so much."

"Right. Your legend is already made, Mr. Adams. In other words, you've reached your peak."

Clint sat back in his seat and said, "Well, that was relatively painless."

"Frankly, I'm surprised."

"Why?"

"Well . . . people with reputations like yours usually have egos to match."

"Sorry," Clint said, "no inflated ego here."

"I was also surprised that you tried to argue that kid out of drawing his gun."

"Sometimes it works."

"And you prefer that to killing?"

"Oh, yes," Clint said, "definitely. Killing just isn't as much fun as it was years ago, you see."

"Now you're making fun of me."

"Sorry," Clint said. "It's just that I can probably count on the fingers of one hand the men I've known who actually *like* to kill."

"Maybe I could write about them."

Clint smiled.

"Most of them are dead, I'm afraid."

"Killed by you?"

Clint waggled a forefinger at Bonney.

"We don't want this to start sounding like an interview, do we?" Clint asked.

"Oh," Bonney said, closing his notebook and putting it away, then showing Clint his empty hands, "no, no interview, I promise. I don't do interviews unless they're agreed to."

"Never made one up?"

"Never."

"Well," Clint said, "that makes you unusual, doesn't it?"

"I suppose it does," Bonney said. "There is something you might be able to help me with, though."

"Why don't you get yourself a drink—on me, of course—and then we'll talk about it."

"Fair enough."

"Oh," Clint said, "and while you're at the bar you can get me another beer, too."

"But you told the sheriff—"

"The sheriff doesn't have to know I had another one, does he?"

"No," Bonney said, standing up, "I don't suppose he does."

FOUR

Bonney came back to the table with two beers and put one in front of Clint.

"It's on me," he said, seating himself once again.

"Thanks. Now, what is it you'd like me to help you with?"

"I'm looking for a man," Bonney said, "and I think maybe you can help me find him."

"Why are you looking for him?"

"I want to write about him."

"Why?"

"Because he's a legend in the making."

"I see," Clint said. "What makes you think I could help you find him?"

"I just thought, well, since you're something of a legend yourself . . ."

"Send a legend to find a legend?"

"Something like that."

"Well, I don't agree that I'm a legend, but maybe before I give you my answer you should tell me who we're talking about."

"He calls himself Wild Bull Hanson."

Clint wasn't sure he'd heard right the first time. Actually, he was hoping he hadn't.

"Say that again?"

"Hanson," Bonney said, "Wild Bull Hanson. Have you heard of him?"

"No," Clint said, "I can't say that I have. Tell me about him."

"Well, we've heard about him in the East. I wonder why you haven't?"

"I travel a lot."

"That must be it," Bonney said. "Well, he's said to have killed twenty-two men in fair fights."

"Impressive . . . to anyone who's impressed by those kinds of statistics."

"Well, my readers are."

"That's too bad. I don't think I can help you, Mr. Bonney."

"Well, wait now," Bonney said, "let's not be too hasty. If you haven't heard of him, maybe you know someone who has."

"I might."

"Good, then we can do business."

"Are you proposing that I help you for money?"

"Well, I'm sure my publisher would pay you well for your help, yes."

Clint was trying to hold his temper, but it was getting more difficult by the moment.

"Why do I sense that you're . . . not happy about something?" Bonney asked.

"Probably because you've got good instincts."

Bonney sat back in his chair.

"What's wrong?"

"I'll tell you what's wrong," Clint said. "James Butler Hickok was a friend of mine."

"Hickok—you mean, Wild Bill?"

"Yes, Wild Bill," Clint said, "and I don't appreciate someone trying to cash in on his name after he's dead."

"Hickok died years ago."

"He was *killed* years ago."

"But . . . the names aren't even the same," Bonney said. "There's Hickok and then Hanson. They don't even sound alike."

"Wild *Bill*," Clint said, "and Wild *Bull*?"

"Oh," Bonney said, "that's your problem."

"Maybe you're not as unusual a newspaperman as I thought," Clint said.

"What's that supposed to mean?"

"You don't see anything wrong with one man trying to trade off a dead man's reputation?"

"I don't see that that's the case here, Mr. Adams," Bonney said. "Honestly."

"Well, then, we see the situation a lot differently."

"Well, then, I guess that means you'll help me."

"How do you figure that?"

"Well, you're going to want to set this right, aren't you?"

"You're not going to get anywhere trying to manipulate me, Mr. Bonney," Clint said.

"But—"

"I'm afraid our discussion is over," Clint said firmly. "I'd appreciate it if you'd finish your beer at the bar, or at another table."

Bonney stared at him for a few moments, then slid his chair back and stood up.

"No, that's okay," he said. "I don't have to finish it."

"Suit yourself."

"I'll be at the hotel, if you change your mind, Mr. Adams."

"I won't," Clint said, "and I'm leaving town right after this beer."

"If you'll excuse me for saying so," Bonney commented, "that's what you said about the last beer."

Clint simply stared at Bonney until the younger man began to fidget.

"Well . . . I'm sorry we can't . . ."

The newspaperman left without finishing his statement, which suited Clint just fine.

FIVE

When Clint left the saloon he went to the telegraph office instead of the livery stable.

"Can I help you, sir?" the clerk asked.

"Yes," Clint said. "What's the nearest town with a telegraph office?"

The man smiled a friendly smile and said, "We got a pretty nice one right here, sir."

"I realize that," Clint said, "and I'm going to use it, but I'll have to get my reply somewhere else. Can you help me with that?"

"I understand," the man said. "Yes, there's a telegraph office in Emma."

"Emma?" Clint asked. "That's a town?"

"Yes, sir."

"How far is it?"

"About . . . twenty miles."

"That'll do," Clint said. "Thanks."

"Would you like to send your telegram now?"

"Yes, I would."

The man gave him a pencil and paper, and Clint wrote a telegram to his friend Rick Hartman, in Labyrinth, Texas, asking for any information he might have on a man who was calling himself Wild Bull Hanson.

"Looking for Bull Hanson, huh?" the clerk asked as he read the message over.

"You've heard of him?"

"Sure," the man said. "You haven't?"

"No."

"Supposed to have killed over twenty men."

"Twenty-two, I heard," Clint said. "Where have I been that I haven't heard of this fella?"

The clerk shrugged and said, "I'll send this message now."

"Thank you."

Clint paid the man and left the office. This time he went directly to the livery stable and saddled Duke, his big black gelding, himself. Ordinarily he would have stopped at the livery for some supplies, but since Emma was only twenty miles away he felt sure they'd make it before nightfall.

He paid the liveryman what he had coming and then rode Duke out of the stable and out of town, grateful to be leaving it behind. He hadn't even stopped to find out the name of the young man he'd killed. What was the use in knowing their names, after all this time?

Instead of thinking about the dead man he was thinking about the newspaperman, Bonney, and the man calling himself Wild Bull Hanson. He really didn't have any intention of getting involved. His request to Rick Hartman was just to satisfy his idle curiosity.

Of course, he was a man whose curiosity did not stay idle for long.

• • •

After Clint Adams rode out of town D. L. Bonney went to the telegraph office to talk to the clerk.

"I can't tell you that, sir," the clerk replied to Bonney's request. "I can't tell you what the gentleman sent."

"Okay, then," Bonney said, putting some money on the counter, "if you can't tell me what he sent, can you tell me who he sent it to?"

The clerk eyed the money sadly and said, "No, sir, I can't tell you that, either."

"Okay," Bonney said, "one last try. Can you tell me where he was headed when he left here?"

Suddenly the clerk smiled and snatched the money from the counter.

"That I can tell you, sir."

A half hour after Clint Adams left Springfield for the town of Emma, D. L. Bonney left, heading for the same place.

SIX

Clint rode into Emma before dark. It was a small town, so small that he was surprised that it even had a telegraph office. He left Duke at the livery and went to the Emma Hotel to get a room.

"Sure, we got rooms," the clerk said. "This ain't exactly Dodge City, or didn't you notice?"

"I noticed it's a little small," Clint said. "Who's Emma?"

"Damned if I know," the clerk said. "What room do ya want?"

"I get my pick?"

"Sure."

"Room five."

"Ya got it," the man said, and handed him the key.

Clint went up to his room, which smelled so musty it must have been uninhabited for months. He dropped off his saddlebags and rifle and then went back downstairs to find the telegraph office.

"Nope," the clerk said, "nothin' come in for Clint Adams." The man peered at him suspiciously and asked, "Is that you?"

He was a wizened little old man with a face that looked as if it had collapsed in on itself.

"Yes, that's me."

"The Gunsmith, right?"

"Yeah, that's right."

"What the hell you doin' in Emma?" the man asked. "This place is a pimple."

"I'm just passing through."

"And waitin' for a message?"

"That's right."

"From where?"

"Labyrinth, Texas."

"Never heard of it."

"I guess that doesn't matter, does it?"

"I guess not."

"This town got a saloon?"

"It's got one," the man said, holding up one crooked, wrinkled finger.

"Well, when my reply comes in I'll either be at the Emma Hotel or the saloon . . . whatever it's called."

"It's called the Emma Saloon," the old man said, "but mostly we just call it the saloon."

"Okay," Clint said, "then I'll either be at the saloon or the hotel."

"You want I should run it over there for ya?"

"If you can."

"I look like I got any run left in me?" the old man asked.

Clint looked at the old man for a few moments and said, "How about if I just check back in from time to time?"

"That's a might good suggestion."

Clint nodded and said, "Thanks."

He left, spotted the saloon across the street, and crossed over to it.

D. L. Bonney rode into Emma about an hour behind Clint. He rode down the main street and saw that the town had one hotel, one saloon, and a telegraph office. Most likely Clint Adams had registered at the hotel, stopped into the telegraph office, and was now in the saloon.

Bonney turned his horse around and rode back to the livery.

"Anybody ride in ahead of me?" Bonney asked the liveryman.

"Yep."

"One man?"

He took a moment to spit some tobacco juice into the dirt and then said, "Yep."

"What'd he look like?"

The man shrugged.

"Where's his horse?"

Now the man's eyes lit up.

"Big black gelding back here."

That was Adams's horse, Bonney knew.

"You and him ridin' in," the man said, "it's like a population explosion."

"Not many people come through here, huh?"

"Not when they can stop at Springfield," the man said. "I mean, why stop here when you can ride two more hours and be in Springfield?"

Bonney couldn't answer that, so he didn't try.

"Tell me something."

"What's that?"

"This town have a newspaper?"

"Why would it?"

"Why does it have a telegraph office?"

The man shrugged.

"I guess somebody wanted it."

"One more question."

"Go ahead and ask."

"Who's Emma?"

The man shrugged, spit some more tobacco juice, and said, "Damned if I know."

SEVEN

D. L. Bonney registered at the hotel, left his gear in his room, and then found a chair and sat in front of the hotel. From his vantage point he could see the front of the telegraph office, and the saloon was just down the street. He'd walked down to the saloon just long enough to peer in the window and see Clint Adams sitting at a table with a beer. He didn't know if he'd gotten his reply yet, but thought that if he had he wouldn't be sitting in the saloon in the town of Emma, just doing nothing.

Bonney had an idea what Adams's message had been about, anyway. He was probably looking for information on Wild Bull Hanson.

Bonney had played dumb with Clint Adams. He knew why the man had been upset. Certainly Wild Bull was trying to cash in on Wild Bill's name. Anybody who didn't recognize that fact was a fool or an idiot. It was no skin off Bonney's nose, though, and it made for an even better story—or it would, once he found Hanson.

His tip that Hanson was in Springfield had been a bust, but he'd been lucky enough to run into Clint Adams. Just because Adams had refused once didn't mean that Bonney was going to stop trying. He had to bide his time, though.

Clint finished his beer and left the empty saloon to go back to the telegraph office. The same wizened old man was behind the counter.

"Did that reply come in yet?" he asked.

The old man looked up at him and said, "Just come in a minute ago." He handed the reply to Clint.

"Thanks," Clint said, and started out.

"Ain't ya gonna read it?"

"I am," Clint said, "over another beer."

He took the reply back to the saloon with him, ordered another beer, reclaimed his table in the empty room, and read the reply.

CLINT,
HAVE HEARD STORIES ABOUT HANSON STOP DON'T KNOW WHETHER OR NOT TO BELIEVE STOP MAYBE YOU CAN TELL ME WHAT YOU FIND OUT STOP

RICK

Clint put the telegram down on the table. It wasn't a big help, but at least he knew that Rick had heard of the man. Now he was even more curious about him.

As if right on cue, the batwing doors opened and D. L. Bonney walked in. He walked to the bar, got himself a beer, and walked directly to Clint's table.

"Mind if I sit?"

"As long as you don't try to tell me that this is a coincidence."

"No," Bonney said, "no coincidence."

"Good," Clint said, "I hate coincidences."

"I found out you were headed this way," Bonney said. He indicated the telegram on the table and asked, "What did you find out?"

"Not much."

"What do you think?"

"I think," Clint said, "that you think you're manipulating me, but you're not."

"I don't think I am."

"Yeah, you do," Clint said. "See, you're the type of young man who thinks he's smarter than everyone else."

"You don't even know me."

"I know your type."

"And what type is that?"

"I just told you," Clint said. "You're a smart young man, Bonney, but you're not as smart as you think you are."

"You're probably right," Bonney said.

They sat there and sipped their beers in silence until Clint spoke.

"I'm going to help you find this Hanson fella."

"Good," Bonney said. "Do I get to ask why?"

"Because I want to talk to him."

"Just talk to him?"

"That's all."

"Why don't I believe you?"

"What does it matter why I want to help you?" Clint asked.

"Well . . . it doesn't . . . not really."

"Fine."

"So . . . when do we start?"

"Tomorrow."

"What about today?"

"I'll send out some more telegrams," Clint said, "see what I can find out."

"Maybe we can get something to eat," Bonney said.

Clint looked around at the room, which was still empty but for them and the bartender.

"Not here," he said.

"No, probably not."

"While I go back to the telegraph office you find some-place to eat."

"Why can't I come with you? We can ask around for a restaurant."

Clint just stared at him.

"Oh, I get it," Bonney said. "You don't want me to know who you're sending telegrams to. Okay, I can re-spect that. God knows I don't like to give up my sources."

They both stood up.

"I'll find us a place to eat."

"Meet me in front of the hotel in half an hour," Clint said. "Maybe I'll have some information."

EIGHT

Clint sent telegrams to everyone he could think of, starting with Talbot Roper, his private detective friend who lived and worked out of Denver. He asked essentially the same question he had asked Rick Hartman: Had he ever heard of a man called Wild Bull Hanson? He left the Emma location for the reply.

He proceeded to send telegrams to others, like Bat Masterson and Luke Short, hoping that he knew where they were and the telegrams would get to them.

Still others went out to people whose locations he was sure of, such as lawmen and newspapermen and women he knew. All were given the Emma location and asked to reply as soon as possible.

"This office is havin' its best day ever," the old clerk said.

"And it's all because of your winning personality."

"Huh?" the man said, but Clint was out the door already.

"I found a place," Bonney said as Clint joined him in front of the hotel.

"Good," Clint said, "I'm hungry."

"What did you find out?"

"Nothing, yet."

Bonney opened his mouth to ask another question, but Clint beat him to it.

"Where is this restaurant?"

"It's this way," Bonney said. "The desk clerk said we couldn't miss it."

"How could you miss anything in this town?" Clint asked. "You've heard about a one-horse town?"

"Yeah."

"This is it, I'll bet."

They walked a ways, past the saloon and telegraph office, until Bonney said, "I think that's it."

A sign above a doorway said: RESTAURANT.

"What was your first hint?" Clint asked.

They entered the place and found it empty.

"The rush must be over," Bonney said.

"I smell food," Clint said. "Let's get a table."

They took a table against the wall, and Clint sat so he could see the whole room.

"You really do that, huh?" Bonney asked, sitting across from him.

"Do what?"

"Sit with your back to the wall."

"When I can."

"I thought . . ."

"You thought what?"

"I thought that was just part of the myth."

"So's getting shot in the back," Clint said sourly.

"Like Hickok, huh?"

Clint glared at him.

"How can you be so smart, and yet try to pretend you're so stupid."

"I'm sorry . . ."

"I suspect that the truth is somewhere in the middle," Clint said. "Am I right?"

"Probably," Bonney said. "I guess I do have a high opinion of myself."

"A good opinion of yourself is healthy," Clint said. "A high opinion, though, could get in the way."

"It hasn't yet."

"Fine," Clint said. "Maybe it never will. I wish you luck."

A waiter finally appeared and looked at them in surprise.

"Never seen customers before?" Clint asked.

"Not two strangers," the man said. "Could take me a while to recover."

"Can you make us a couple of steak dinners while you're recovering?"

"Comin' up."

As the waiter left, Bonney said, "I have something I want to say."

"Say it."

"I understand how you feel about your friend, Hickok," Bonney said. "I don't mean to demean that. I'm just trying to get to a story."

"Any story?" Clint asked. "Or a true story?"

"What do you mean?"

"You've heard stories about this Hanson." He couldn't bring himself to say "Wild Bull."

"Yeah."

"Do you want to add to the stories, the so-called legend, or do you want to find out if it's true?''

"I want to know if it's true."

"And if it isn't?''

"If it isn't, then I'll print that."

"Are you sure?''

"I said it, didn't I?''

"You'll excuse me, Mr. Bonney," Clint said, "but I don't know you well enough to know what your word is worth."

"Let me get this straight," Bonney said. "You want to be sure that if Wild Bull Hanson is a phony, that's the story I'll print?''

"That's what I want."

"I give you my . . ." Bonney started, then stopped short. "Well," he said, after a moment, "I can promise, but I guess you'll just have to wait and see."

"I guess I will," Clint said.

NINE

After they finished eating, Clint allowed Bonney to accompany him back to the telegraph office where they collected about half a dozen responses to his telegrams.

"What do they say?"

"They're real similar," Clint said, reading them quickly while standing just outside the telegraph office. "Bat Masterson has heard of Hanson but has never met him. The same for Talbot Roper."

"The detective?"

"That's right."

Bonney seemed more impressed that Clint knew Roper than Bat Masterson.

"And the others?"

"The same," Clint said.

"No one knows where to find him?"

Clint shook his head.

"This is going to be harder than I thought," Bonney said.

"What made you think it would be easy?" Clint asked.

"I don't know," Bonney said, shaking his head. "I thought a man with a reputation would be relatively easy to find."

"Well, you thought wrong," Clint said.

"Obviously. What do we do now?"

"There are still some telegrams that might bring in some replies. I suggest we stay here for the night and worry about what to do in the morning."

Bonney looked up and down the street and said, "It looks like we'll also have to worry about what to do tonight."

Since they only knew each other in the town of Emma they could either stay in their rooms, sit at separate tables in the saloon, or spend the time together. They decided that since they were going to be riding together for a while they should probably get to know each other better.

They met at the saloon after going back to their respective rooms for a short while, and Clint brought a deck of cards.

"Do you play poker?" Clint asked.

"No," Bonney said.

"Never?"

"Never have."

Clint frowned, then began to deal out a hand of solitaire. He had often found that playing poker with someone gave him insight into the personality of the man. Did he play his hand close to the vest? Did he bluff? These questions, he'd found, often revealed a man's character.

He'd have to get to know D. L. Bonney better without the benefit of poker.

"Tell me some of the things you've written," Clint said.

"Oh, nothing you would have seen."

"We do get eastern newspapers out here from time to time," Clint said. "Especially in Denver and San Francisco."

"Do you spend a lot of time in those cities?"

"I have spent time there, yes," Clint said. "I've also been to Boston and Philadelphia and New York."

"Really?"

"Yes."

"Then maybe you have seen some of my work."

Bonney proceeded to reel off the names and subjects of some articles and essays he'd written, but Clint had heard of none of them. Eventually, Bonney was eyeing him suspiciously, thinking that he might have been set up.

"Do you know many writers?" Bonney asked.

"Some."

"Like who?"

"Well . . . I know Mark Twain."

That made Bonney sit up and take notice.

"Tell me about him. Where did you meet him? What's he like?"

Clint proceeded to tell Bonney about meeting Twain—whose real name was Samuel Clemens—on a riverboat on the Mississippi, and then again running into him in Boston, when they were both working for the same publisher.

"Wait a minute," Bonney said. "You had a publisher?"

"I almost did."

"For what?"

"He wanted me to write my life's story."

"And you did?"

"I started to," Clint said, "but then I decided that my

life's story was mine and I didn't have to share it with anyone if I didn't want to.''

''So you didn't write it.''

''No.''

''Do you think you ever will?''

''I might,'' Clint said, ''but then that doesn't mean I'd let it be published.''

They suspended conversation while Bonney went to the bar for two more beers. It was later in the day now, and the saloon was busier than it had been all day. That meant that, other than Clint and Bonney and the bartender, there were about three more men in the place.

''Tell me, what do you want to write eventually?'' Clint asked.

''What makes you think I'm not happy doing what I'm doing?''

Clint smiled.

''Nobody's happy doing what they're doing,'' Clint said. ''That's just the way life is. Come on, what do you want to write?''

Bonney hesitated, then said, ''I want to write novels, great novels.''

''What makes a great novel?''

''The story has to be important, and it has to touch people.''

''What about Twain's work? Is it important?''

''Yes, and it touches everyone. That's what's wonderful about his work. Also, the work of Robert Louis Stevenson.''

''I met him on a train once,'' Clint said.

''Truly?''

''Why would I lie?'' Clint asked. ''It was a very brief meeting, though.''

''Any others?'' Bonney asked. ''Have you met any other writers?''

"None as famous as those," Clint said. "Perhaps in a few years I'll be telling people that I met you when you were young."

"I hope so," D. L. Bonney said.

"Do you think writing about someone like this Hanson fella is going to get you where you want to be?"

"Writing about Hanson is just a job," Bonney said. "My publisher is paying my way, and it's an opportunity to see the West."

Clint couldn't argue with that. He was of the opinion that a man should see as much of the country—and the world—as he could, and he said so.

"I've never been out of the country," Bonney said. "Have you?"

"I have."

"Where have you been?"

"I've been lucky enough to travel to Australia, South America, and England."

"I would love to go to England," Bonney said.

"Oh," Clint said, "and Canada."

"I've not even been to Canada."

"Well, that should be your first stop, then," Clint said. "Either that or Mexico. They're the easiest foreign countries to get to."

"I haven't even been to Mexico."

"Well, you'll have to go," Clint said, "and get your publisher to pay your way."

"I'll just have to figure out a way to do that."

"That should be simple," Clint said. "Just tell him that Hanson is in one of those places."

Bonney bit his lip.

"You mean lie?"

"You are a newspaperman, aren't you?" Clint asked.

"But I don't lie," Bonney said.

"Then maybe you aren't cut out to be a newspaper-man."

"Do you believe that all newspapermen lie?" Bonney asked.

"It's been my experience."

"What about all writers?"

"Well," Clint said, "what is a novel except one big lie?"

"Fiction!" Bonney said. "Not a lie. Fiction is not a lie."

"All right, granted," Clint said, putting a red queen on a black king, "that's story telling."

"That's right."

"It's funny."

"What is?"

"When you're young and you tell stories, you're considered a liar," Clint said. "When you grow up and do it, you're considered a writer."

Bonney laughed.

"And you get paid for it," he added.

"That's right," Clint said. "I forgot about that. I guess you'll just have to write a great novel, get paid for it, and then travel with all the money."

"And write other novels."

"It sounds like the perfect life."

"It will be."

"Except for one thing."

"What's that?"

Clint gathered up all the cards and began to shuffle them.

"Somewhere along the line you should learn how to play poker," Clint said.

"Why?"

"It's an important tool in assessing people."

"Really?"

"Well, I have found it to be such."

Bonney studied Clint's hands while he shuffled the cards, and then he asked, "Will you teach me?"

"Why not?" Clint said. "What else have we got to do?"

TEN

"Think this town has a sheriff?" Bonney asked.

"Most towns have a sheriff," Clint said.

"Can I bet?"

"You're high on the table."

They had gotten some stick matches from the bartender and were using those to play poker with.

"I bet four," Bonney said.

He had a pair of kings on the table, and Clint suspected he had another in the hole. Clint had an ace on the table, and two in the hole. The writer was about to get a lesson in being too confident.

"Your four," Clint said, "and four more."

Bonney looked at him.

"That's that bluffing you were telling me about," he said.

"You have to pay to see."

Bonney rubbed his jaw.

"How many more cards do we have coming?"

"Seven," Clint said, "this is seven-card stud."

"Oh, right," Bonney said. "Okay, I . . . call?"

Clint nodded. Bonney tossed in the other four match sticks.

"Last card," Clint said, and dealt it, watching Bonney's face. Of course, this was no contest. Almost every card showed on the younger man's face. Clint could see that the man's hand had not improved, so he most likely had three kings.

Clint looked at his hole card and it was a deuce. He had another deuce on the table, so he now had aces full. There was no way Bonney could beat him.

"It's your bet," Clint said.

"Five," Bonney said, and hastily tossed them into the pot.

"Your five," Clint said, "and ten more."

"Ten?"

Clint nodded.

"More bluffing," Bonney said, but Clint did not respond.

Bonney threw five sticks in, hesitated, then said, "Okay, I raise ten more."

He started to count ten more out, but when he got to nine he had none left.

"Can I make that nine?"

"Sure," Clint said.

"Okay, then," Bonney said, "I raise nine."

Clint put his nine in and said, "I call, because you're tapped out."

"You mean if I had more match sticks you'd raise?"

"That's right."

"I—I've got three kings," Bonney said. "That's pretty good, isn't it?"

"That's very good," Clint said, "ordinarily."

He spread his cards to show his full house.

"Wow," Bonney said, shaking his head. "Did you just get one of those aces?"

"No," Clint said, raking in the sticks, "I had the three aces early. I knew I had your three kings beat."

"You knew I had three kings?"

Clint nodded.

"My face again?"

"Yes."

"Damn," Bonney said. "How do you keep your hand from showing on your face?"

"It takes a lot of practice," Clint said. "Want to keep playing? I'll loan you some more sticks."

"No," Bonney said, "I owe you three million or so, as it is. We can continue the lesson another time. I think I'm going to turn in."

"Good night, then."

"How about you?"

"I'll stay up a little longer," Clint said, then spread his hands. "Who could sleep with all this going on?"

Bonney looked around and said, "Yeah, I guess . . ."

As the younger man walked out, Clint wondered if he'd ever develop a sense of humor.

ELEVEN

D. L. Bonney went back to his room, kicked off his boots, removed his shirt, and settled down on the bed with his notebook. He started writing down everything he could remember Clint Adams saying during the course of the day. He had no intention of betraying Clint's trust, but he wanted to have everything down in writing, just in case.

In the saloon Clint sat back in his chair, looking around for somebody to play poker with, this time for real money. He couldn't believe that the saloon in any town could be this empty at this time of night, except for a ghost town—and he knew this wasn't a ghost town.

He guessed he'd been right when he told Bonney this was the quintessential one-horse town.

Bonney had been gone a half hour when the batwing doors swung open and a man walked into the saloon. It was the wizened old man who ran the telegraph office. Clint watched as the man walked to the bar and ordered a beer. He waited a few moments, then got up and walked up to the bar.

"Close the office?" he asked.

The old man looked at him.

"What's it to ya?"

"Just thought I'd buy you a beer and make some conversation," Clint said.

"Man wants to buy me a beer, Ed."

"Two bits," the bartender said. He looked to be in his fifties.

Clint paid him.

The telegraph operator looked around the saloon and then cackled.

"This damn town," he said, "is almost dead, did ya notice?"

"How could I not?" Clint asked. "Is the saloon always this empty?"

"Always," the old man said. "Ain't gonna change, either. We're done for."

"Why don't you leave?" Clint asked.

"Man wants to know why we don't leave, Ed," the old man said.

"Where would we go?" the bartender asked.

"Don't know," the old man said. He looked at Clint and asked, "Where would we go, mister?"

"Well . . . Springfield?"

The old man cackled.

"They got a telegraph operator already."

"And a bartender," Ed said.

"Then go someplace else."

"Everyplace else is the same," the old man said. "They're all dying."

"What?" Clint asked.

"Every town is dying."

"Some of them are just popping up," Clint said, "just being born."

The old man shrugged over his beer.

"They'll die, eventually."

"What about Denver?" Clint asked. "Or San Francisco? Surely they have enough jobs to go around for a bartender and a telegraph operator."

"Too many people," the old man said. "Besides, where else could I go where I could be the telegraph operator and the mayor?"

Clint stared at the man.

"You're the mayor?"

"Hell, yes," the old man said, "and Ed, here, is the sheriff."

Ed reached beneath the bar, brought out his badge, showed it to Clint, then put it back beneath the bar.

"Well, then, I guess you fellas are where you want to be."

"I guess," the old man said and cackled again.

"Well," Clint said, "I guess I'll turn in, then . . . unless you've got some women around?"

The mayor snorted.

"Or some men who like to play poker?"

Ed, the bartender/sheriff, shook his head.

"To bed, then."

As Clint turned away from the bar, the mayor said, "Hey."

"Yes?"

"You might want to take this with you."

"What's that?"

Clint turned and the old man took something out of his shirt pocket.

"This." He offered Clint a piece of paper.

"What's that?"

"One more reply."

Clint took it and opened it, read it, and then folded it and put it in his pocket.

"Thanks."

"Guess you'll be leaving in the morning," the old mayor said.

"Looks like it," Clint said. "Will we be able to get breakfast before we leave?"

"Same place you got dinner tonight," Ed said.

Clint looked at Ed and asked, "How do you know where we ate?"

The old man cackled and said, "He's the sheriff, ain't he?"

TWELVE

In the morning, over breakfast, Clint showed Bonney the telegram.

"What's this?"

"The telegraph operator gave it to me in the saloon last night."

"What does it say?"

"Read it."

Bonney did so, and raised his eyebrows.

"New Mexico," he said, handing it back.

"Uh-huh." Clint took the telegram back and put it in his pocket.

"Is your source good?"

"Very reliable," Clint said. "I've known Owen Judd for a long time."

"How long will it take us to get to New Mexico?" Bonney asked.

"That depends," Clint said.

"On what?"

"On how well you can ride."

Bonney swallowed and said, "Ride?"

"You rode here, didn't you?"

"Well, yeah," Bonney said, "and my butt is killing me."

"I never would have guessed."

"Everything doesn't show in my face, like in poker, Clint."

"Well," Clint said, "New Mexico is a long way from here. Are you willing to ride all the way?"

"For a story," Bonney said, "I'll ride from here to . . . well . . ."

"New Mexico," Clint said, "is as far as you'll have to go."

After breakfast they went to the livery to look at Bonney's horse.

"Did you buy this animal?" Clint asked.

"I rented it," Bonney said. "I'll have to take it back."

"We're not going back that way."

"But . . . the horse isn't mine."

"You can be grateful for that," Clint said. "I'm surprised this horse made it this far."

"What do I do then?"

Clint put his hands on his hips.

"I doubt that this town has a horse for sale that could make it to New Mexico," Clint said. "You'll just have to ride this one to the next town. Maybe we can get a better horse there."

"What is the next town?"

"Don't know," Clint said. "We'll just have to mount up and find out."

• • •

They walked their horses back to the hotel, checked out, then mounted up and started out of Emma.

"Not much of a town," Bonney said.

"Might have been, once."

"You think so?"

Clint shrugged.

"Might be something to write about."

"What do you mean?"

"The life and death of a town," Clint said. "Do you think that might be something people would want to read about?"

Bonney seemed to be thinking about it.

"Maybe," he said finally, "you know . . . maybe." They were outside of town by then. Bonney looked back over his shoulder and asked, "What was the name of that town again?"

"Emma," Clint said. "For some reason they called it Emma."

THIRTEEN

By the time they reached New Mexico—the town of Branton, to be exact—Clint wondered if Hanson—he couldn't bring himself to use the rest of the man's so-called name—was even in the state anymore.

Bonney had proven to be not only a bad rider, but a terrible one. They had to constantly stop for him to rest, and the longer they rode, the worse he seemed to get. The trip wouldn't have taken half as long if he hadn't repeatedly insisted on stopping.

"Jesus," Bonney said as they rode into town, "I thought we'd never make it."

"Me, too," Clint said.

"Okay," Bonney said, "so I'm not the best rider in the world, but I'm probably not the worst."

Clint didn't reply.

"Am I?"

Clint looked at him.

"Worst I've ever seen."

"Well, I'm sorry," Bonney said. "It's not something they taught in college."

"Oh," Clint said, "You went to college. That explains a lot."

"Like what?" Bonney's tone was belligerent.

"Take it easy," Clint said. "I'm just joking."

"Oh," Bonney said, then added, "I don't have much of a sense of humor, in case you haven't noticed."

"I noticed."

After an awkward silence Bonney asked, "What do we do now that we're here?"

"We'll take care of our horses, get rooms, and then find Owen Judd. He'll tell us if Hanson is still here or not."

"Do you think he is?"

"No."

"Me neither," Bonney said, "not after all this time."

"Well, maybe Owen will know where he went," Clint said. "We have to get you off that horse, though."

"I'd appreciate it."

They had bought Bonney a new horse at the very next town after Emma, a town called Kendall. It wasn't much larger than Emma, but it had more life, and it had some decent horses for sale.

Now they rode to the livery, where they turned Duke and Bonney's new horse over to the liveryman.

"How many hotels have you got in this town?" Clint asked.

"Two," the man said. "One new hotel. It's got a real nice dining room."

"Where are they?" Bonney asked, rubbing his butt.

"We passed one on the main street," Clint said.

"You passed 'em both on Main Street," the liveryman

said. "The new one sort of looks more like a theater."

"Why is that?" Clint asked.

"To make it look fancy."

"But people might go right by it, thinking it's a theater."

"Maybe it says hotel in front?" Bonney said.

"No," the liveryman said, "it says New Branton House."

"Which could mean anything," Clint said. "I think we'll go to the old house—I mean, hotel."

"Suit yourselves."

They did. They left the livery and walked to a building that said simply BRANTON HOTEL. They got two rooms, then left the hotel and walked to the office of the *Branton Chronicle*.

Owen Judd had been editing newspapers for most of his life. He was now forty-four years old and had been at the helm of the *Chronicle* for the past five years. In that time, Branton had doubled in size.

As Clint and Bonney entered the office, the printing press abruptly came to a halt. It was a coincidence, but Clint had always found it hard to concentrate in a room with the press running.

"Owen?"

Owen Judd turned and his face brightened when he saw Clint. He was a tall, gangly man with one big jug-handled ear. The other ear was a crushed mess, the result of an accident when he was a reporter trying to get a story. Maybe that was how he managed to put up with the noise of the printing press.

"Clint, boy!" Owen Judd said. He hurried across the room and shook hands. "You're late. I expected you long ago. Hanson's gone."

"I figured as much," Clint said. "We couldn't exactly expect him to stay around and wait for us."

"Do you know where he went?" Bonney asked.

Judd looked at him.

"Oh, I'm sorry," Clint said. "Owen, this is D. L. Bonney. He's a writer from back East. He's looking for Hanson."

"Oh?" Judd said. "Why?"

"To, uh, write about him."

"Why don't you write about Clint?" Judd asked. "He's much more interesting."

"Clint won't, uh, allow me to write about him."

"Uh, also," Clint said, "it appears I've been written about enough."

"Is that a fact?" Judd asked.

"That's what Bonney tells me," Clint said. "Seems the people back East have read their fill of me."

Judd looked at Bonney again.

"What's the D. L. stand for?"

"How'd your ear get like that?" Bonney asked.

Judd stared at the younger man for a few moments, then poked him in the chest with his forefinger and said, "I guess we can talk about all of that at dinner."

"And Hanson?" Clint asked.

"I've got some ideas about that," Judd said, "but I really need to get this edition done. Can you come back at five?"

"Sure," Clint said, "we'll be back."

"Fine," Judd said. "See you then."

Clint and Bonney went outside and stopped on the boardwalk.

"We've got four hours to kill," Clint said.

"Does this town have a whorehouse?"

"I suspect it does," Clint said. "At least, it did the last time I was here."

"Yeah," Bonney said, looking up and down the street, "but will it look like a whorehouse?"

"Mr. Bonney!" Clint said, as if surprised.

"What?"

"I do believe you made a joke."

"I did?" Bonney asked, frowning.

FOURTEEN

Bonney thought it was strange that Clint didn't want to go to the whorehouse with him.

"Why not?" he asked.

"Because I don't pay for sex."

"Why not?"

"I don't have to."

"Well . . . me neither, but sometimes I get busy, you know?" Bonney said. "I need the . . . release without having to do the, uh . . ."

"Work?"

"Right."

"Have a good time, then," Clint said. "I'll be in one of the saloons—most likely the Red Branch, if it's open."

"Okay, then," Bonney said. "Meet you there at four?"

"Four, it is."

Bonney nodded, and they split up.

• • •

Clint was happy to see that the Red Branch was open for business. As he entered, the place was half filled. This was a welcome change from towns like Emma and the not-much-better Kendall. Thriving towns were like a tonic to Clint. He fed off the energy.

It was early and there were no girls working the saloon. That suited Clint. He'd be looking for a girl later. Now all he wanted was a beer.

He walked to the bar and ordered one, then took it to a table that gave him a vantage point of the whole room. He had not been in Branton for three years, maybe more, so there was no reason to expect that he'd remember anyone, or that anyone would remember him. He'd only been there to see Judd, and only for a couple of days, but even then he had drank in the Red Branch and had found a saloon girl willing to sleep with him just for the enjoyment of it.

He sipped the beer slowly and thought about the ride to New Mexico with D. L. Bonney. The man was worse than a child, constantly complaining about his discomfort. Clint wondered if he wanted to ride any further with the man. Maybe he should just go off on his own and find this Hanson fella. He'd put off making that kind of a decision until they had dinner with Judd and heard what he had to say. For now he'd sit tight, enjoy a couple of beers, maybe a few hands of poker, and wait until four.

D. L. Bonney picked out a plump brunette and followed her up to her room, enjoying the way her rounded ass swayed from side to side. He liked his women with some meat on them, and usually picked them in their early twenties.

When they got to her room she turned and undid the single tie that held her nightie together. It fluttered to the floor, leaving her completely naked. Her breasts were big and round, with dark brown nipples, and her hips and thighs were a little fleshy.

"Am I okay for you?" she asked.

"You're perfect for me."

"Some men like skinny women."

"Well," Bonney said, "I picked you, so I guess I don't like skinny women."

She sat on the bed and watched as he undressed.

"Did you just get to town?"

"That's right."

"And I'm the first person you're talking to?"

"Sure," he said.

"I'm flattered."

He discarded the last of his clothes.

"You have a nice body."

"Don't," he said.

"What?"

"You don't have to compliment me, or say nice things. I'm paying for this, so let's just do it."

His penis was rigid and ready, and she licked her lips as she looked at it.

"Actually," she said, "you do have a nice body, whether you're paying me or not. Also, I like to talk to strangers, because I like to hear about places I haven't been."

Bonney sighed. Why was he like this with women? he wondered.

"I'm sorry," he said. "I . . . sure, we can talk some."

"Honey," she said, standing up from the bed and approaching him, "we can talk a lot . . . but we can talk while we're doing other things."

She took his penis in her hands, cupping it there lightly.

"Do you like anything fancy?" she asked.

"That depends on your definition of fancy."

She dropped to her knees and said, "If I get too fancy, you let me know."

Bonney wondered for a moment how she expected to talk when she was doing *that* . . . and then stopped thinking.

Bonney spent an hour with the whore, whose name was Debbie. She never did get to anything that was too fancy for him.

Clint remained in the saloon the whole time, nursing two beers and then finally getting into a small poker game with three of the townspeople. At that time he stopped drinking, because he never mixed gambling and drinking.

By the time Bonney showed up at the saloon, Clint had won four times what Bonney had spent for an hour with Debbie.

"Time to go, gents," Clint said, as he spotted D. L. Bonney entering the saloon.

"So soon?" one man said.

"Will you give us a chance to get our money back?" another asked.

"What would you use, a gun?" the third man asked.

"Gents," Clint said, "if I'm around town you'll all have your chance—if you want it."

"I don't want it," the third man said. "If I play you again I'll just lose more money."

"No wonder you always lose," the first man said. "You got no confidence . . ."

Clint didn't hear any more because he moved away from the table and met Bonney at the bar.

"You look relaxed," he said.

"I am," Bonney said. "I had this incredible girl—"

"I don't need the details, thanks," Clint said.

"What else have you got to do?" Bonney demanded.

Clint eyed the man, then said, "You're right—but let's get a beer before you start telling me all the gory details."

FIFTEEN

"...and this will amaze you," Bonney said. "After that she took me in her—"

"That's it, I'm afraid," Clint said.

"What do you mean?"

"Time's up," Clint said, pushing away from the bar. "We've got to go and meet with Owen."

"Hey," a man leaning on the bar said, "we want to hear about it."

It was then that Clint and Bonney realized that several men at the bar had been eavesdropping on their conversation.

"Don't worry," Clint said to them, "he'll come back later and tell you the rest. Come on."

They left the saloon and walked over to the newspaper office, where Owen Judd was already locking up.

"Ah, there you are," Judd said. "Come on, I'm starved."

"Lead the way," Clint said.

"Who do you write for, Mr. Bonney?"

"I freelance quite a bit, selling articles to different publications."

"Somebody's paying you for this trip, though," Judd said.

"Of course."

"Ah," Judd asked, "who?"

"Why would you want to know that?" Bonney asked.

"Professional curiosity."

"Well . . . I think I'll keep that to myself, for the time being."

"Why?" Clint asked.

"Because your friend, here, is a writer, too," Bonney said, "and if I tell him who's interested in my story, what's to stop him from doing it himself and getting there ahead of me?"

"Owen wouldn't—"

"I would if I could," Judd said, cutting Clint off. "That is, I might have done it in my younger days, Clint. Leave the lad alone. He doesn't have to answer my questions."

"Thanks," Bonney said.

"Forget it," Judd said. "We newspapermen have to stick together."

Judd took them to a café halfway between the newspaper office and their hotel.

"You mean you're not staying at the brand-new Branton House?" he asked as they were seated by a waiter.

"A little too fancy for me, Owen," Clint said.

"Too fancy for the whole town, if you ask me," Judd said.

"The town seems to be growing, though," Clint said. "Maybe it will grow into the place."

"I hope not."

62   J. R. ROBERTS

"Are you against prosperity, Mr. Judd?" Bonney asked.

"I'm against it coming too fast, Mr. Bonney."

"You know, a man recently told us that all towns are dying."

"We're *all* dying from the moment we're born," Judd said, "why not a town?"

Judd told them the only thing that the restaurant knew how to cook well was eggs in the morning and steak in the evening.

When the waiter came over they all ordered steak.

"Okay, Owen," Clint said, "tell me about Hanson."

"Wild . . . Bull . . . Hanson," Judd said slowly, for effect.

"Oh, please . . ."

"No, no," Judd said, "the man's impressive, Clint. He looks the part."

"What's that mean?"

"Long hair, mustache—"

"Christ," Clint said, cutting his friend off, "he's even stolen Bill's look?"

"Bill . . . oh, I see now why you're interested," Judd said. "The name . . . you didn't know what he looked like?"

"No."

"Just heard the name."

"From Bonney, here," Clint said. "I'd never heard of the man before that, but apparently a lot of people have."

"That's what happens when you move around the way you do, Clint," Judd said. "You never get the chance to sit and read a newspaper."

"Newspapers are depressing," Clint said. "They all print bad news."

"That's not true—" Bonney started.

"Oh, don't try to convince him, lad," Judd said. "Let

him think what he wants. You and I know the truth.''

"Which is?" Clint asked.

"Newspapers are the heart and soul of this country,"
Judd said.

"The eyes and ears," Bonney said.

"The conscience."

"The voice!" Bonney said.

"Right!" Judd said.

"Bull!" Clint said.

"Here's the food," Judd said. "I'm starved. Can we
table this discussion until after dinner?"

"What about Hanson?" Bonney asked.

"After dinner," Judd said.

"But—"

"Eat," Clint said. "The sooner we start, the sooner
we're finished, and then we'll get what we want."

SIXTEEN

"Never had a lick of trouble while he was here," Judd said. "The man never even drew his guns in anger."

"Guns?"

"He wears two," Judd said.

"Not in a sash, I hope."

"No," Judd said, "in holsters."

"Tell us more."

"He was charming," Judd said. "Told stories to the children, tipped his hat to the women, even the men listened to him talk."

"What about the law?"

"What about him?" Judd asked. "Sheriff Wilcox is a good man. He talked to Hanson as soon as he got to town, and then that was it. There was never any reason to talk to him again."

"He didn't kill anybody?" Bonney asked, sounding disappointed.

Judd laughed.

"You're a bloodthirsty little son of a bitch, ain't you?" He clapped a hand down on Bonney's left shoulder. "You're probably gonna make a good newspaperman, Bonney."

"Thanks . . . I think."

"What did you think of him, Owen?" Clint asked.

"What can I say?" Judd said. "The man made good copy while he was here, Clint."

"And how long was he here?"

"He stayed a couple of weeks."

"And you wrote about him?"

"Every other day," Judd said, "and then before he left I did an interview."

"I'd like to see what you wrote," Clint said.

"I would, too," Bonney said, then added, "if it's okay with you."

"Hell, yes, why not?" Judd asked. "After all, I write for people to read, don't I? We can go back to the office after coffee."

As if on cue, the waiter brought out a large pot of coffee and three cups. He filled them and left.

"Do you believe his legend, Owen?" Clint asked.

"Do I believe anyone's?" Judd asked. "Do I believe yours?"

"You know me."

"I also know that legends are blown up reputations, and they're blown way out of proportion."

"Is that true?" Bonney asked Clint. "Is your reputation blown out of proportion?"

"I don't know," Clint said. "I never listen to what people say about me."

"You don't? Why not?"

"It makes me . . ."

"What?" Bonney asked. "Angry? Embarrassed? Ashamed?"

"Yes," Clint said.

"Yes to which one?"

"All of 'em, kid," Owen Judd said, as Clint looked away, "all of 'em."

SEVENTEEN

To D. L. Bonney's credit he did not pursue the matter with Clint. Instead, they finished their coffee and followed Owen Judd back to his office.

"Have a seat at that table," Judd said, pointing. "I'll bring the material out to you."

While Judd was in the back finding the appropriate editions, Bonney asked, "Is he married? Does he have a wife we're keeping him from?"

"He's only married to his job," Clint said.

"Here we go," Judd said, reappearing with an armful of newspapers. "I've only got one copy for both of you, so you'll have to take turns."

"I'll take the interview," Bonney said.

"All right," Clint said, "I'll look over the rest of the stuff."

"And I've got some typesetting to do for tomorrow," Judd said.

"Not about me, I hope," Clint said, without looking up from the papers.

"I know better than that, Clint," Judd said, "don't I?"

"I hope so."

Judd moved away from them, and again Bonney whispered a question.

"How'd his ear get like that?"

"I did it."

"You did?"

Clint nodded.

"The first time he ever wrote about me without clearing it with me first."

Bonney stared at Clint for a few moments, then asked, "That's a joke, right?"

Clint turned his head and looked at Bonney.

"Yeah, kid," he said, "it's a joke. You want to read that so I can read it when you're done?"

"Oh . . . sure . . ." Bonney said, still unsure as to whether or not Clint was, indeed, kidding.

Clint read all of the articles on Hanson, but they didn't tell much. They were basically "A Day in the Life of a Gunman" stuff, and there was nothing interesting there, because the man didn't do anything interesting while he was in town.

After Clint switched with Bonney, he started reading the interview. This was better. There was some stuff here where he actually talked about men he had killed. Still, there was no proof.

"You fellas finished?" Judd asked, coming up behind them.

"Owen," Clint said, "did you believe all of this stuff he was telling you?"

"What does that matter?" Judd asked. "I have to believe what I'm writing to write it?'' Judd looked at Bonney. "Tell him, kid."

"Tell him what?" Bonney asked. "I believe what I write."

"Yeah, right," Judd said. "You're gonna write about Wild Bull Hanson and just believe everything he tells you?"

"Well, no," Bonney said, "I'm going to check out what he tells me."

"Everything?"

"Everything I'm going to write about, yes."

"Kid," Judd said, slapping Bonney on the shoulder, "I wish you all the luck in the world in this business, with an attitude like that."

"But what—"

"Come on, are you done?" Judd asked. "I've got to get some sleep."

"How late is it?" Clint asked.

"It's too late for this newspaperman," Judd said. "I got to get back here at six a.m."

"Do you want us to help you clean up?" Clint asked, as he and Bonney stood up.

"No, I'll clean up in the morning," Judd said. "Just get your asses out of here so I can lock up."

They all stepped outside and waited while Judd locked the door.

"How long will you be in town?" Judd asked.

"That depends on your answer to our next question," Clint said.

"Which is?"

"Where did Hanson go from here?"

"What's the difference?" Judd asked. "He won't be there anymore when you get there, either."

"Just humor us," Clint said.

"Okay," Judd said. "He told me he was heading north."

"Colorado?" Clint asked.

"That's what he said."

"But where?"

Judd shrugged.

"He didn't mention a town."

"Not even one?"

"Well . . . wait a minute," Judd said. "He did mention a girl, and he said . . . that she was . . . in . . ."

"Come on, come on . . ." Bonney said.

"Edgewater," Judd said. "The town of Edgewater."

"Is that in Colorado?" Clint asked.

"I don't know," Judd said, "but since he said he was going to Colorado, it's a good bet."

"Okay," Bonney said enthusiastically, "thanks."

"Then again," Judd said, "the whole thing could've been a lie."

"Thanks, Owen," Clint said, extending his hand. "We'll be leaving first thing in the morning."

"It was good to see you, Clint," Judd said. "What are you gonna do to Hanson when you catch up to him?"

"I don't know," Clint said. "Maybe I'll make him prove he is what he says he is."

"You're gonna call him out?"

Clint made a face.

"I don't even like that term," he said. "It makes it sound like I want to go on a damned picnic with him or something."

"Okay," Judd said, "don't tell me. I'll probably read about it in a newspaper. Hell, maybe the kid here will write it up."

Judd extended his hand to Bonney, who shook it.

"I meant what I said inside, kid," he said. "Good luck."

"Thanks, Owen."

They went their separate ways, Judd home and Clint and Bonney in the general direction of the saloon and the hotel.

"What are you going to do now?" Bonney asked.

"Get some sleep, and I suggest you do the same," Clint said. "I want to get out of here early tomorrow."

"Maybe I'll just go over to the whorehouse again," Bonney said, "just for a little while."

"Suit yourself," Clint said, "but if you're not up in the morning, I'm leaving without you."

"Don't worry," Bonney said, "you're not going to get rid of me that easily."

EIGHTEEN

In the morning Clint rose and went downstairs to check out. He carried his gear with him to the hotel dining room and ordered breakfast. He was halfway done with his meal when D. L. Bonney appeared, looking harried and not at all rested. He also had his gear with him, indicating that he had checked out.

"Sorry I'm late," he said, sitting across from Clint.

"You're not late," Clint said, "I'm early. You have time to have breakfast."

"Good," Bonney said, "I'm starved."

The waiter came over and Bonney ordered the same thing Clint was having, steak and eggs.

"Did you have an interesting night?"

"Interesting," Bonney said, "that's a good word for it. Want to hear about it?"

"No," Clint said. "I don't even know why I asked about it."

The waiter brought Bonney's breakfast, and Clint had a second pot of coffee while the other man ate.

"You drink a lot of coffee," Bonney observed.

"I like it," Clint said.

"You always drink it black?"

"And with no sugar," Clint said. "That's the way coffee was meant to be drank."

Bonney made a face and added cream to his coffee.

"What's our next move?" he asked.

"Our next move," Clint said, "is to get your butt back in a saddle."

"It's okay," Bonney said. "I'm not so sore."

"Good, because I've made a decision."

"And what's that?"

"If you can't keep up this time," Clint said, "I'm going to leave you behind."

"That's your decision?"

"Neither one of us will ever catch up to Hanson if we have to keep stopping so you can rest."

"I'll be fine," Bonney said. "I'll keep up, don't you worry."

"Fine," Clint said. "Then we don't have a problem, do we?"

"No," Bonney said, "we don't."

"Good."

There were a few moments of awkward silence while Bonney ate, and then he said, "It's not like I do it on purpose."

"I never said you did."

"I'm just not used to all this riding, is all."

"Well," Clint said, "after this you will be."

NINETEEN

Jimmy Tappia stared across the room at his brothers, Billy and Jesse. Of the three, Jimmy was the oldest, Billy the middle, and Jesse the youngest. However, while Jimmy had always been the oldest and Jesse had always been the youngest, Billy hadn't always been the middle brother. That's because there used to be four. Bobby had been the second oldest, but now he was dead.

Jimmy, Billy, and Jesse Tappia wanted the man who had killed him—Wild Bull Hanson.

"Tell me," Jimmy said.

Billy and Jesse wanted to tell him what they had found out, but they were busy looking past their brother at the woman in the bed. She was a tall brunette, lean the way Jimmy liked his women, with small, high breasts the size and firmness of slightly overripe peaches.

"Billy!"

Jimmy's tone snapped Billy out of his spell.

"He's on his way here," Billy said.

"Hanson?"

Billy nodded.

"How do you know that?"

"He was spotted."

They were in the town of Zackel, Colorado.

"He's on his way here?" Jimmy asked. "To this town?"

"Uh, no," Billy said, "we heard he's on his way to Colorado, but we don't know if he's coming here."

"It's been four months since Bobby was killed in Leyburn," Jimmy said. Leyburn was another Colorado town, the one in which Bobby Tappia had been gunned down. "Now he's finally coming back to Colorado?"

"That's what we heard," Billy said. Then he nudged his brother Jesse and said, "Right?"

"Uh, right," Jesse said, without taking his eyes from the brunette.

She was reclining naked on the bed, apparently unconcerned that there were two more men in the room than she'd bargained for. Actually, she found Jesse the cutest of the three, although it was Jimmy who had brought her up here. In her early thirties, she found her taste in men running to the young ones like Jesse Tappia, who didn't appear to be any more than twenty.

"Billy," Jimmy said, "I want you to . . . no, wait. I'll get dressed and come with you."

"To do what?"

"Send some telegrams," Jimmy said, grabbing his clothes.

"To where?"

"I'll tell you on the way."

Behind his back the brunette licked her lips and crooked a finger at Jesse.

"Uh, do you need me, Jimmy?" Jesse asked.

"To send some telegrams?" Jimmy asked, pulling on his boots. "Naw. Why?"

"Uh . . ."

Jimmy sat up and looked behind him at the brunette, who smiled.

"Oh," he said, then looked at his younger brother. "Think you can handle her?"

Jesse shuffled his feet and said, "I think so." His penis was already hard, just at the thought of trying.

"Well, go ahead, then," Jimmy said, standing up. "She's already been paid."

Jimmy turned and looked again at the woman, who—he couldn't help but notice—had one leg in the air and her hand down . . . there.

"You don't mind, do you, sweetheart?"

"I don't mind at all, Jimmy," she said.

"Just don't hurt him, okay?" Jimmy said to her.

"I'll only bite him," she said, "a little."

As Jimmy went past Jesse, he slapped his brother on the shoulder and said, "And don't hurt yourself, little brother."

As his brothers left, Jesse was glad he'd taken a bath that morning.

TWENTY

"You're pretty," the woman told Jesse Tappia.

"Aw," he said, "I ain't. You're the pretty one."

"Okay," she said, playing with her long black hair, twirling it around one finger, "we're both pretty. Come here."

Jesse moved closer to the bed and the brunette sniffed the air.

"You had a bath today, didn't you?"

"Yes."

She got on her knees and started to unbutton his shirt. He couldn't take his eyes away from her hard brown nipples.

"I like the young ones like you," she said, sliding one hand into his shirt. "Especially when they're clean."

"Um," he said, as she tweaked one of his nipples.

"Do you know how many smelly, dirty men I see in a week?"

"Um," he said again, "a lot."

"A whole lot. Are you a virgin?"

"Huh?"

"You ever been with a woman before?"

"Oh, yeah, sure I have."

"Ever been with a woman who wasn't a whore like me?"

"Um, twice."

"Same girl?"

He nodded.

"Who?"

"A girl back home."

"How old was she?"

"Sixteen."

"How old were you?"

"Sixteen."

She finished unbuttoning his shirt and slid it off of him, letting it drop to the floor. He was skinny, not scrawny, and he had smooth skin. She bent her head and licked one of his nipples, then the skin around it. He closed his eyes and tried to keep from groaning.

Most of the whores he'd been with had just lain on their backs and opened their legs for him. When he was sixteen and he did it twice with Charlene Matthews, he hadn't known what he was doing and neither had she.

This gal knew what she was doing.

She put one hand over his cock through his pants, sort of measuring him and weighing him.

"Oooh," she said, "I'll bet you got a nice little pecker—well, not so little. What's your name again?"

"J-jesse."

"Jesse, I'm Elaine. Let's take off your pants and find out how big you are, huh?"

"Uh," he said, his voice squeaking a bit, "s-sure."

•   •   •

Jimmy and Billy left the Zackel Hotel and walked to the telegraph office.

"Who do we know between here and the border?"

"A few guys," Billy said.

"Well, gimme their names, and where they are."

"Well—"

"Wait until we get inside and you can write them down," Jimmy said. "I don't have a great memory like you do, Billy."

"Uh-huh."

Billy cursed his memory. It was because he remembered things so well that things like this happened to him. Here he was walking in the street with Jimmy while Jesse was up in the room with that whore. Sure, Jesse was the good-looking one and the whore had liked him, but Billy would have at least liked a chance with her, especially since she was already paid for.

"Thinkin' about that whore?" Jimmy asked.

Billy looked embarrassed.

"Well, yeah . . ."

Jimmy pushed his brother's hat down further on his head.

"When we're done here I'll buy you your own, how's that?"

"Well . . . sure."

"And she won't be skinny," Jimmy said, "like Elaine. I know you like girls with more meat on them."

"And red hair."

"It just so happens there is one with red hair," Jimmy said. "When we're done here we'll go and get her, okay?"

"O-okay, Jimmy," Billy said. "Whatever you say."

TWENTY-ONE

Jesse Tappia stood before Elaine, totally naked.

"Oh, my," she said, "you *are* a pretty one."

"I'm not—"

"And I'll bet you're sweet, too."

She got off the bed and lowered herself to her knees before him.

"Mmmm," she said, licking him. "Oh, yes." She licked him again, a long lick along the underside of his penis, and then she opened her mouth and took him inside. "Mmmmm, yes," she said, releasing him, "you *are* sweet. You have the sweetest—"

Jesse didn't hear what else she said. The blood in his ears was roaring too hard, and he was afraid he was going to explode all over her.

"Oh, no," she said, sliding her thumb and forefinger down to the base of his penis and tightening them there, like a ring. "Not yet, my sweet boy. I'll let you mess me

80

up later, but not yet, not until I'm through with you.''

This was a switch, Elaine Walker thought. Usually, as the whore, she was the one who was used, but this boy was like a present to her, and she was going to use him, not the other way around.

''I have plans for this pretty thing,'' she said, swiping at the swollen head of his penis with her tongue, ''and it has to stay hard, huh?''

She released his penis and stood up. She was an inch or so taller than him, something else she liked. She walked around him, looking at him from all angles.

''Mmm,'' she said, touching his buttocks, ''you have a nice butt, did you know that?''

He swallowed and said, ''Nobody ever mentioned it before.''

''Well, mark my words,'' she said, rubbing her hands over his ass, ''someone will. Mmmm . . .''

''What?''

She slid the middle finger of her right hand along the crack of his ass.

''I was just wondering . . .''

''Wondering what?''

''If you're as sweet back here as you are in front,'' she said. She slid her finger down so that she touched his anus. He started, as if struck by a tiny jolt of lightning. No one had ever touched him there.

''You ever have your ass licked?'' she asked.

He opened his mouth to speak but nothing came out.

''I didn't think so,'' she said, laughing.

She lowered herself to her knees again and began to kiss his buttocks, first one side, then the other, tiny little kisses that felt good and caused him to get the chills. Finally, she used both hands, spread his ass cheeks, and gently probed with her tongue.

"Oooh," he said, shifting his feet but not moving away from her.

Why would he want to move away from *that*?

"Here," Billy said, handing his brother a piece of paper. "These are the names and the towns where they are."

"Good," Jimmy said.

"Are you gonna send Ma a telegram, too, Jimmy?" Billy asked.

"Why?"

"She must be wonderin' when we're gonna come back," Billy said. "She can't run the ranch alone."

"I know, Billy," Jimmy said. "We can't go back until we get the bastard who killed Bobby. Ma would kill us herself if we did, you know?"

"I know."

"But I'll send her a telegram," Jimmy said. "I'll let her know what we're doing, okay?"

"Okay, Jimmy," Billy said. "I know you'll do what's right."

"I always do," Jimmy said, "don't I?"

"Yeah, you do."

"Okay, then," Jimmy said. "Why don't you wait for me outside while I send these telegrams."

"And then we'll go to the whorehouse?"

"Yep," Jimmy said, "then we'll go and get you that redhead."

Jesse Tappia had never been in this position before. He had always been on top of the whores, not them on top of him—and he was on his belly. This woman seemed to just love rubbing herself on him, like she was doing now.

She had licked his ass for a while, using her fingers, too, saying she was screwing *him* with her wet finger, and as long as it felt good and nobody was looking, where was the harm?

Then she had told him to lie down on his belly, and she started rubbing her body all over him. Her nipples were hard, but her skin was so soft and smooth.

"Do you like this, my sweet boy?" she asked, her mouth right next to his ear.

"Yes, but—"

"But what?"

"W-when do I get a chance to touch you?"

She spread his legs so she could slide her hand beneath him and take hold of his hard penis.

"You don't like me touching you?" she asked.

"It ain't that," he said. "It's just, well, I'm the man."

"You're my sweet boy, aren't you?" she asked.

"Well, I ain't—"

She released his penis and took hold of his testicles tightly.

"Hey!" he protested.

"You're my sweet boy," she asked again, "right?"

TWENTY-TWO

When Jimmy Tappia came out of the telegraph office, his brother Billy turned and looked at him hopefully.

"It's a good thing Pap had friends all over, Billy," Jimmy said. "Our friends along the borders are going to keep watch for Hanson."

"Which borders?"

"All of them," Jimmy said. "If he comes into Arizona or leaves it, we'll know."

"Can we go to the whorehouse now?" Billy asked.

"Sure," Jimmy said, "let's go. We'll get you that redhead."

"And what about you?"

"I got a paid-for whore in my hotel room, remember?" Jimmy asked. "That is, if our little brother hasn't killed her by now."

Of course, when he said it, it was a joke.

• • •

Jimmy left Billy at the whorehouse with a busty red-head and went back to his hotel. When he walked into the room he was stunned by what he saw.

Jesse Tappia was sitting cross-legged on the floor, naked. On the bed the brunette whore, Elaine, lay with her neck at an odd angle.

"Jesse?"

Jesse looked up at his brother.

"It wasn't my fault, Jimmy."

"Jesse . . . what did you do?"

"It wasn't my fault."

Jimmy walked to the bed and looked at the woman. He didn't have to touch her to know that she was dead.

"Jesse . . . what happened?"

"It wasn't my fault."

Jimmy knelt next to his brother.

"I know it wasn't your fault, Jesse," he said. "I'm not saying it was. I just want to know what happened."

"She hurt me."

"How did she hurt you?"

Haltingly, Jesse told Jimmy most of what had happened—he left out the part about the woman shoving her finger up his ass—and finished by telling his brother that she had grabbed ahold of his balls.

"It hurt," he said. "I told her to stop but she just kept askin' me, 'Are you my sweet boy, are you my sweet boy?' "

"And then what happened?"

"I told her yeah, I was her sweet boy."

"And then what?"

Jesse looked at Jimmy, his face streaked with dried tears.

"I don't remember, Jimmy," he said, "I really don't."

"Jesse," Jimmy said, "you killed the girl. Her neck is broken."

"It's not my—"

"I know, I know, it's not your fault," Jimmy said, "but . . . you killed her and you don't remember?"

Jesse shook his head.

"She hurt me, Jimmy," he said. "You ever have a girl do that to you?"

"No," Jimmy said, "but I can imagine how it must have hurt."

"W-what do we do now?" Jesse asked.

"That's easy," Jimmy said. "We get out of town before somebody realizes what's happened. Come on, get up."

He helped his brother to his feet.

"Are we leavin' right now?"

"First we have to get you dressed," Jimmy said, "then we have to get the body out of my room. Then we have to collect your brother, and *then* we'll leave."

"It really wasn't my fault, Jimmy," Jesse said, sniffling.

"I know, Jesse," Jimmy said, patting his brother's shoulder, "I know."

TWENTY-THREE

"This is hopeless," D. L. Bonney said.

Clint looked at him across their camp fire. They each had a plate of beans in their lap and a cup of coffee on the ground next to them.

"What is?"

"Finding Hanson."

"Why is it hopeless?"

"We don't know where he is!"

"Bonney?"

"Yeah?"

"That's why we have to find him," Clint said, "because we don't know where he is."

"I know that."

They had ridden for two days, and Clint told Bonney they'd be in Colorado tomorrow.

"All we have to do is track him," Clint said.

"You know how to do that?"

"I know several different ways."

"Is it hard?"

"It'd be easier if we had an actual warm trail to fol-low," Clint said. "What we're following now is a trail of words."

"Words?"

"We have to depend on *hearing* where he's been, or where he's going to."

"Like hearing he was in New Mexico?"

"Right," Clint said, "and he was there. We just arrived too late."

"Because of me?" Bonney's tone was defensive.

"No," Clint said, "he probably would have been gone anyway. We missed him by a full week, remember."

"Oh."

"I'm not going to blame you, Bonney," Clint said. "You've done well since we left Branton."

"I have?"

"I don't think you'll ever be a great horseman," Clint said, "but you've done all right."

After a few moments of silence Bonney asked, "So you think we'll find him?"

"We'll find him," Clint said. "A man with a reputation can't hide for long."

"You sound like you've tried."

"I have," Clint said, "more than once. It can't be done."

Another silent patch, this one broken by Clint.

"Listen," he said, "do I have to keep calling you Bon-ney? Don't you have a first name?"

"Sure."

"Good," Clint said. "What can I call you?"

"D. L."

"I thought—"

"That's my name," Bonney said. "D. L."

Clint stared at him.

"Your parents called you D. L.?"

"That's right."

"Why would they do that?"

"They couldn't agree on a name," Bonney said, "but they liked the sound of D. L., so . . . that's it."

"D. L.," Clint said, trying it out.

"Right."

Clint thought about it, then shrugged and said, "Well, it's better than Bonney."

When dinner was over Clint cleaned out the plates and put them away, but he left the cups out and made another pot of coffee.

"Not for me," Bonney said when Clint poured himself a fresh cup.

"Why not?"

"Do you always make it so strong?"

"I always make it the same way," Clint said. "It's the way I like it."

"Well . . . one cup's enough for me. I'm going to turn in."

"I'll finish this cup and turn in, also."

"Don't we have to—I don't know—stand watch or something?"

"Why?"

"I don't know," Bonney said. "I just thought . . . that's what you did out here. You know . . . stand watch?"

"Only when there's a reason, D. L.," Clint said. "Go to sleep and don't worry. We're safe."

Bonney wrapped himself in his blanket and rolled over. Clint found himself wishing he could read something that D. L. Bonney had written. He seemed awfully naive for someone who claimed to be a writer.

TWENTY-FOUR

The Tappia brothers had a problem now that they had left the town of Zackel. All of the telegrams Jimmy Tappia had sent had that town listed for a reply.

"We've got to find another town with a telegraph office," Jimmy said.

Billy did not reply. He'd been quiet ever since he heard what Jesse had done to the whore in Zackel.

"What for?" Jesse asked.

Jimmy told him that they needed someplace to get their replies.

"Why not home?"

Home was a ranch in northern Arizona.

"I don't want to go home yet," Jimmy said. "Not until we've taken care of Bobby's killer."

"No," Jesse said, "I mean the telegrams can go home, and we can get the replies from there, also by telegraph."

Jimmy looked at his younger brother.

"Jesse," he said, "I didn't know you had it in you. That's a great idea."

"T-thanks, Jimmy," Jesse said proudly.

"Ain't that a grand idea, Billy?" Jimmy asked.

"Sure."

"Why didn't you think of that?"

"I ain't that smart."

"A really fine idea, Jesse," Jimmy said again.

Over the course of the next few days Clint and Bonney passed through half a dozen towns. Clint would talk to the local sheriff about strangers with a reputation—yes, he said too many times, like me!—while Bonney talked to the local newspaperman.

This brought them to the town of Zackel.

"A damned shame," the sheriff said to Clint.

His name was Dale Long. He was in his fifties and was incensed by the murder of a whore that had happened just under a week ago.

"Anybody under suspicion?" Clint asked.

"Well," Long said, "we did have three strangers in town, brothers, but they didn't have reputations."

"What were their names?"

"Tappia," the lawman said. "One of them was called Jimmy. I don't know the other two."

"How do you know about the name Jimmy Tappia?"

"Well," Long said, "the strangest thing . . . he sent a bunch of telegrams, and then left the same day before the answers came in."

"Sounds like they left in a hurry."

"That's what I thought," Long said. "Something made them leave real sudden-like, but I can't prove nothing."

"It's a shame," Clint said.

"A damn shame. Funny you should ask about somebody with a rep, though."

"Why's that?"

"The telegrams he sent? They were asking people about a feller named Wild Bull Hanson. Ever heard of him?"

"Yes, I have, Sheriff," Clint said, "but only recently."

"Well, seems like the Tappia boys are looking for Hanson."

"Do you know why?"

"No . . . but why does anybody look for a man with a rep? Hey, you could answer that one, huh?"

He could have, but he didn't.

"Thanks for your help, Sheriff."

"Sure."

"I wish I could help you with your problem."

"Hey," Long said, "a lot of the town don't think it's a problem. It's just a dead whore, you know?"

"I'm sorry, Sheriff," Clint said, "but I don't understand that kind of thinking."

"Nah," Long said, "me neither." He shook his head. "It's a damn shame."

TWENTY-FIVE

Clint met up with Bonney on the street.

"I couldn't find out anything," the writer said, "but I did hear about some dead whore."

"That's what I heard, too," Clint said, "but it's all connected, D. L."

"How?"

"Let's get a beer and I'll tell you."

They went back to one of the saloons Bonney had just come from. It was early, and not many of the tables were taken. Clint grabbed two beers from the bar, and when he turned he saw that Bonney had grabbed a corner table and left him the inside chair.

Over the beer Clint explained about the Tappia brothers.

"Have you ever heard of these brothers?" Bonney asked.

"No."

"Why do you think they're looking for Hanson?"

"There could be a lot of reasons," Clint said, "but let's concentrate on two."

"And they are?"

"One, they're looking for him because he has a reputation."

"And two?"

"Revenge."

"For what?"

"Who knows?" Clint said. "But when you have a reputation, somebody is always looking for you for revenge. Maybe . . ."

"Maybe what?"

Clint had stopped short as a thought occurred to him.

"Maybe Hanson killed a member of their family," he said. "Another brother, perhaps."

"What are you thinking?"

"We've got to find the telegraph office."

"More telegrams?"

"It's an invaluable tool, D. L.," Clint said. "You of all people should know that. One of these days you'll be sending your stories back East that way."

"It would take a key operator forever to do that," Bonney scoffed.

"Maybe," Clint said, "but this time I only need to send one line."

"To whom?"

"A friend of mine in Labyrinth, Texas. If there's anything to know about the Tappia brothers, he'll know it."

"He didn't know much about Hanson, did he?"

"That's what makes me think there isn't that much to know," Clint said.

"What do you—"

"Finish your beer and let's go," Clint said, draining his.

• • •

They walked to the telegraph office and Clint sent off his question, asking for an immediate reply. That reply said: TAPPIAS FROM NORTHERN ARIZONA STOP FATHER A BIG RANCHER STOP SONS LAYABOUTS AND TROUBLEMAKERS STOP FOUR SONS, ONE DEAD IN GUNFIGHT STOP HANSON?

Rick Hartman was thinking along the same lines as Clint. If the Tappias thought that Hanson had killed their brother they'd be looking for him.

There was one more line to the message: TAPPIA SENIOR, DECEASED, LEFT BEHIND A LOT OF FRIENDS STOP LUCK STOP RICK

All the Tappia brothers had to do was tap into the ring of friends their father had left behind.

"They're tracking him the same way we are," Clint said, putting Rick's reply in his pocket.

"By stories they hear?"

"Right," Clint said, "and it looks like they've got a lot more ears out there than we do."

"So what do we do?"

"That's easy," Clint said. "We start tracking the trackers."

"Huh?"

"We follow the Tappia brothers," Clint said. "They should lead us to Hanson."

"How do we follow them?"

"According to the sheriff," Clint said, "one of those brothers killed that whore. They left here about three days ago, heading east. We should be able to pick up their trail fairly easily."

"Ah," Bonney said, "this is that other kind of tracking you were telling me about."

"Right," Clint said. "At least we have a tangible trail to follow, left by the Tappias."

"When do we get started?"

"We get started now," Clint said.

"Aren't we going to stay in town overnight?"

Clint put his hand on Bonney's shoulder.

"We still have a few hours of daylight left, D. L., and we're going to take advantage of them."

"I saw some pretty women in town . . ." Bonney complained.

"There are pretty women all over the West, D. L.," Clint said. "Don't worry. You'll have your fair share."

TWENTY-SIX

Before leaving the town of Zackel, Clint got an idea.

"Back to the telegraph office," he said.

"Now what for?"

"I'm thinking," Clint said, "that it might be useful to find out who the Tappias sent telegrams to."

"Why?"

"Because maybe we'll find the name of a friend of a friend in there."

"That would be a coincidence, wouldn't it?" Bonney asked.

"Yes, it would," Clint said, "and although I don't usually like or trust coincidences, in this case I'd accept one."

They went to the office and asked the clerk about the telegrams.

"I don't have any."

"Don't you usually keep copies?"

"For a while," the man said, "but this time the sheriff took them all."

"Then we have to talk to the sheriff," Clint said to Bonney.

Outside, on the way to the sheriff's office, Bonney asked, "Why would the sheriff give us the copies?"

"Because he knows that one of the Tappia brothers killed that girl," Clint said. "He'll do what he can to see that they're brought to justice."

"Why would we go after them for killing a whore in this town?"

"We just have to act sympathetic to the sheriff's problem, D. L.," Clint said, "and see what we can get."

Before going into the sheriff's office, Clint said to Bonney, "Just let me do the talking."

When they left the sheriff's office Clint had a list of names in his hand.

"That was well done," Bonney said, in admiration.

"He's been a lawman for a long time," Clint said. "Whichever of the brothers killed the girl, the others are covering up for him. He hates to see them getting away with it."

"But the way you got him to believe that giving us the names and letting us track them might enable him to bring them to justice."

"I didn't do that," Clint said. "He knows he'll never see them again."

"Then why—"

"Because," Clint said, "as long as they get what's coming to them he doesn't care what it's for. In other words, they might not pay for killing the girl, but as long as they end up paying for *something*."

"If they find Hanson and try to face him down, maybe he'll kill them."

"Possible, I guess," Clint said, though he didn't think it probable. Nothing he'd heard about this Hanson indicated to him that the man was on the level. More than once he'd run into men whose legend was in their own minds. If that was the case here, then it was Hanson who would pay when the Tappia brothers caught up to him.

"Now what do we do with the names?" Bonney asked.

"We send them to my friend Rick Hartman and see if he knows any of them."

"And that would be a coincidence."

"Right."

"And we hate that."

"Right again."

"But we'll take it."

"Are you trying to be funny?"

Bonney blinked in confusion and said, "No."

"I didn't think so."

They walked to the telegraph office, entered, and registered the surprise on the face of the clerk, a thirtyish man with a carefully trimmed, pencil-thin mustache.

"You fellers are starting to be my best customers. What'll it be this time?"

"I'll write it out," Clint said.

While he was doing that D. L. Bonney asked the key operater, "Do you think you could send a newspaper story over the wires?"

"I suppose so," the man said. "How long?"

"Pretty long."

"That'd tie up the key for a while," the man said, "and it'd give the feller at the other end of the line a helluva lot to write, but I guess it's possible. You a newspaperman?"

"I am."

"You here about the whore got killed?"

"I'm not, specifically," Bonney said, "but if you know something . . ."

"All I know is that she was a damn good whore," the man said, "but sometimes she got, well, rough."

"Rough?" Bonney asked. "With men?"

The clerk nodded.

"A lot of fellers didn't like that, so she didn't try it with any of the regulars from town. She musta tried it with somebody new, and he didn't like it at all."

"How'd she die?"

"Broke neck."

"I'm ready," Clint said, and handed over the written message.

"Lots of names," the man said.

"Just send it."

"He ain't as talkative as you," the clerk said to Bonney.

Bonney just shrugged and the clerk sent the message on its way.

"We'll wait right outside for a reply," Clint told the man.

"Suit yourself."

Clint and Bonney went outside.

"Did you hear what he said about the dead whore?" Bonney asked.

"I heard. You want to write about it?"

"I would if there was an unusual angle to it," he said. "What about that business about her getting rough?"

"That's not unusual."

"It's not?"

"I've known men who would pay women to be rough with them."

"Really?" Bonney asked. "How rough?"

"Sometimes they'd use whips."

"No!"

"Yes."

Bonney couldn't seem to comprehend that.

"That'd hurt!"

"I think that was the point."

"There are men who like to be *hurt*?" he asked.

"There are men who like to hurt other people," Clint said. "Why not the other way around?"

Bonney just shook his head, and again Clint wondered about the man's naive attitude. He wondered about something else, too. Bonney was supposed to have a publisher who was paying his way, but so far Clint had not seen him wire his publisher for any money. Had he been given that much cash that he had not yet run out?

He was about to ask about this when they heard the loud clacking of the telegraph key. It seemed to go on only for a few seconds and then stop. They went inside.

"Here's your answer," the man said, handing Clint a piece of paper. "Nice and short."

Short wasn't the word for it. The reply was in the form of two words: SAM WATERSTONE.

Clint took out his initial list and saw that Waterstone lived in a town called Weatherby, about two miles ride east of where they were.

"This might be the way they're headed," Clint said.

"That would be a coincidence, too."

Clint looked at Bonney, to see if he was being funny, but got in return a blank stare.

"I guess we better take a ride to Weatherby," Clint said.

TWENTY-SEVEN

Weatherby was a mid-size town that had the smell and feel of a new town. The streets were clean; the buildings were all in one piece, with no peeling paint or warping wood to mar the look of the town. It also had a peaceful feel to it. Even the faces of the people walking the streets were serene.

This town had not seen trouble in a long time, if ever.

Clint and Bonney rode into Weatherby, wondering if they'd find the three Tappia brothers or Wild Bull Hanson, there.

At the very least, Clint hoped, they'd find Sam Waterstone there, and he'd have something useful to tell them.

"This town is different," Bonney said, looking around.

There was hope for the younger man yet, if he was able to feel that.

They rode to the livery stable where a mild-mannered

young man took their horses from them, assuring them that the animals would be well cared for.

"Would you know where we could find a man named Waterstone?" Clint asked.

"Sam Waterstone? He don't live in town."

"Where does he live?"

"He's got a ranch about five miles further east," the man said. "Almost in Kansas. In fact, I think his property extends into Kansas."

"We'll have to ride out there and see him."

"He don't come to town a lot," the man said, "but you never know. He comes once in a while."

"What's he look like?"

"Oh, you can't miss him," the liveryman said. "He's a big man with white hair and a white beard."

"Very tall?"

"No, not tall," the liveryman said, "big." He extended his hands out to show what he meant. Apparently Sam Waterstone was a fat man.

"We'll be on the lookout for him."

"Got business with him?"

"Yes," Clint said, "we've got business with him."

"He's a nice man," the fellow said. "Honest, and a straight shooter."

"Thanks."

They left the livery, and Clint was thinking if Waterstone was so nice and such a straight shooter, why was he friends with the Tappia brothers? Then again, he might simply have been friends with their father.

And, apparently, with Rick Hartman.

"Where to now?" Bonney asked.

"I learned a long time ago that a man's first hour in town is monotony," Clint said.

"What do you mean?"

"You take your horse to the livery," Clint said, "you go and check into a hotel, you leave your belongings in the hotel, you find a saloon, you have a beer to wash away the trail dust, sometimes you have a bath, and then you go about your business."

"A bath sounds good," Bonney said.

"We'll throw that in this time," Clint said, "and since it's getting late, we'll have dinner, as well. If Waterstone appears in town we'll approach him. If he doesn't, we'll just ride out to his place to see him tomorrow."

As they were walking to the hotel they had passed on the way in, Bonney said, "This looks like too nice a town to have a whorehouse."

"You can't control that part of you, can you?" Clint asked.

"Which part?"

"The part that's always looking for a whorehouse."

"Oh," Bonney said, looking down at his crotch, "that part. Can *you*?"

"Usually, I can," Clint said, "but I guess that comes with age."

"I thought when you got older," Bonney said, "that part stopped working."

"You know," Clint said, "if you had a sense of humor . . ."

"What?"

"You'd probably be dangerous," Clint finished. "Come on, let's get the monotony out of the way."

TWENTY-EIGHT

Clint and Bonney were bathed and registered and were having dinner in a restaurant that was near their hotel. The waitress was an attractive woman in her thirties with an extremely pleasant manner.

"Have you just arrived in town?" she asked, smiling at them. Actually, her smile was more for Clint than for D. L. Bonney.

"Just rode in a little while ago," Clint said. "It seems like a nice town."

"It is," she said, "and we always welcome strangers."

"What can you recommend?" Clint asked.

"The beef stew is our specialty," she said.

"Then I'll have it."

"I will, too," Bonney said.

She gave him a smile, but it did not have the same firepower as the one she gave Clint.

"And coffee," Clint said.

"After dinner?"

"Before and after," Bonney said. "He likes coffee."

"And we make very good coffee," she said. "I'll bring a pot right out."

They both watched her walk back to the kitchen.

"Attractive woman," Clint said.

"Too old for me," Bonney said.

"Good," Clint said, "because she's not too old for me."

The waitress's name was Gloria, and she continued to flirt with Clint all through dinner. Finally, it got to the point where Bonney thought he should leave.

"Sounds like a good idea to me," Clint said.

"I'll be . . . around," Bonney said. "I'll take a look at the town, stop in some of the saloons."

"Watch out for yourself."

"I can do that," Bonney said. "I can take care of myself."

"I didn't say you couldn't," Clint said. "I was just reminding you to do it."

"I will, then."

"Fine," Clint said. "I'll see you later, or tomorrow."

"Good luck," Bonney said.

As the younger man left, Clint knew that in addition to looking the town over and stopping at the saloons he would probably also stop by the whorehouse. Clint had never understood the appeal of whores—not when there were women like Gloria around, who were perfectly willing to spend time with a man if he treated them right.

Okay, maybe that *was* the appeal of a whore. She was being paid to do a job, and you didn't have to worry about her feelings.

•   •   •

Sam Waterstone sat in his study at his desk, holding a snifter of fine brandy in his work-roughened hand. When his wife had insisted on buying the stuff he had scoffed, but over the years he had developed a taste for it. Why not drink the good stuff when you could afford it?

He had more on his mind than brandy, however. He'd received a couple of telegrams over the past few days, and they disturbed him.

The first had been from Jimmy Tappia. He did not have much use for the Tappia boys since the death of their father—well, since before the death of their father. They were lazy, shiftless layabouts who, at times, were downright dangerous. Their father had been a fine man, and how he could have spawned four such sons was beyond Waterstone's comprehension. He himself had one son, who had worked side by side with him since he was old enough to ride. Charlie was now his foreman, and he could not have been more proud of him.

He'd heard about the death of Bobby Tappia, though, and had sent his condolences to his mother. Now the telegram he'd received told him that the other three Tappia boys were out for revenge. They were looking for a man named Wild Bull Hanson. A ridiculous name for a man with a ridiculous reputation. Waterstone had seen reputations build in the past, for men like Hickok and Adams and Masterson. It took time, though, and for a man like this Hanson to have built himself a reputation in such a short time—well, Waterstone didn't accept it. Half of any man's reputation was lies anyway. He had a feeling that much more than half was involved here.

The other telegram had been from a man named Rick Hartman. It had taken Waterstone a moment to place Hartman, but when he did he recalled a sound businessman with good sense. Hartman had informed him that Clint Adams might be coming to Weatherby to see him. Hartman had asked that Waterstone give Clint Adams every consideration, as a favor to him.

Of course, Sam Waterstone knew of Clint Adams, but he had never met the man.

Could the two telegrams be connected?

Could the Tappias, Wild Bull Hanson, and Clint Adams be coming together in Weatherby?

And if that were true, could Weatherby stand up to such a meeting?

TWENTY-NINE

Over a second pot of coffee Clint convinced Gloria to let him come back later and walk her home after work.

"I don't usually meet customers after work," she said.

"It's all right," he said. "It's just a walk and some conversation."

Finally she relented. When Clint left the restaurant he had a couple of hours to kill. He decided to look the town over himself and check out some of the saloons.

When he walked into the Weatherby Saloon he found himself in the middle of an altercation between four men. Actually, there were three men on one side and one man on the other—and the single man was D. L. Bonney.

Clint moved to the end of the bar to watch in silence.

"... ain't wearin' no gun," one of the men was saying about Bonney.

"Maybe he's wearin' a diaper," another man said.

"Why would I wear a diaper?" Bonney asked.

"Well, if you ain't man enough to wear a gun," the third man said, "we figure you must be wearin' a diaper."

"Your logic is flawed," Bonney said, and Clint shook his head. Was it possible that the man didn't know he was being teased?

"Come on, friend," one of the men said, "don't that make you mad?"

"Why should I be mad that your logic is faulty?" Bonney asked, sounding puzzled.

The writer's back was to Clint, but he could see the faces of the other three men.

"What's he talkin' about, logic?" one of them asked, looking confused.

"Is he makin' fun of us?" the second man asked.

"I don't know," the third said.

"Gentlemen, I just came in here for a beer and possibly some conversation."

"Well," the first man said, "what if we don't want to conversate with you?"

"That's fine," Bonney said, turning to face the bar, "I'll just drink my beer—"

One of the men grabbed him by the arm and twirled him back around so hard that the contents of his beer mug showered over the three men.

"What the—"

"Jesus—"

"Look what you did."

Bonney stared at the three beer-soaked men and said, "I didn't do it, he did." He pointed to the man who had turned him around. "You made me spill my beer, so I expect you to buy me another."

"What?"

"You expect—"

"He spills beer on *us*," the third man said, "and he expects us to buy him another one."

"Not all of you," Bonney said, "just him." He pointed. "He made me spill it, so he should buy me another. Don't you agree?" The last question was put to the men who were watching the altercation, but none of them had anything to say.

"I agree with you," Clint said.

The three men looked at him, as did the spectators. Bonney turned, saw him, and smiled.

"What?" one of the men asked.

"I agree with him," Clint said, pushing away from the bar and walking toward them until he was standing next to Bonney. "I think you owe this fella a beer, but I tell you what I'll do. In the interest of friendship, I'll stand a round of beers for the four of you. How's that?"

"What if we ain't interested in friendship?" one of them asked.

"Well, what would you be interested in?" Clint asked. "Trying to taunt an unarmed man into a fight?"

"We wouldn't draw on an unarmed man."

"What then?" Clint asked. "A fight, you three against him?"

"He asked for it."

"How did he do that?"

"He come in here unarmed."

"I don't understand—" Bonney began.

"Let me explain it to you," Clint said. "See, these three figure that if you come in here without a gun that means you think you're better than them. You don't *need* a gun. You don't have any respect for them. Do I have it right, boys?"

"Well . . ." one of them said.

"Yeah," another said, "that's right."

"That doesn't make sense," Bonney said.

"No, it doesn't," Clint said, "but there's another possibility, as well."

"What's that?" Bonney asked.

"Yeah," one of the men echoed, "what's that?"

"It's possible," Clint said, "that they're just ignorant asses who are spoiling for a fight, and you looked like a likely candidate because you don't have a gun."

Clint took a quick step forward, and before anyone could move he had taken a gun from the holster of one of the men.

"Hey!" the offended man said.

Clint held the gun out to Bonney.

"Take it."

"What?"

"Take the gun."

Bonney looked at the gun as if it were a live snake.

"I don't want—"

"I know you swore not to touch another gun," Clint said, "but these fellas are asking for it."

"What—"

"Whataya mean," one of them asked, "he swore not to touch a gun?"

"The last time three men picked a fight with him," Clint said, then looked confused and said, "no, it was four—the last time four men picked a fight with him he killed them."

"All four?" one of them asked. It didn't matter which. They had long since become interchangeable.

"That's right," Clint said. "He got so mad that before he knew it they were lying on the floor, and none of them had even cleared leather. And another thing . . ."

Clint leaned forward, and the three men found themselves leaning toward him to make sure they could hear.

". . . he didn't even remember doing it."

Clint leaned back, as did the three men.

"Of course, there were witnesses, and they saw him draw and fire four times, and the four men lay dead. But you know what? They were asking for it, just like you fellas are.''

Clint looked at Bonney again and said, ''Here, take it.''

Bonney just gaped at him.

''Oh, well,'' Clint said and tucked the gun into Bonney's belt. He stepped away and said, ''Okay, boys, have at it.''

THIRTY

"They could have killed me!" Bonney said later.

"I wouldn't have let them kill you."

They were sitting at a table in the crowded saloon, a corner table that two men had given up not in fear of Clint but of D. L. Bonney.

"You gave me a gun!" Bonney said. "I don't know how to use a gun."

"They didn't know that," Clint said. "Besides, I took one of their guns, so it would have only been two against one."

Bonney drank half his beer and put the mug down, breathless.

"I can't believe you did that!" he said. Then he repeated, "They could have killed me."

"Relax," Clint said.

"And that story you told them," Bonney said. "I never killed anyone."

"They didn't know that either."

"Look," Bonney said, "look, everyone in here is looking at me funny."

"Good," Clint said, "then nobody else will bother you."

The three men had backed down rather than face an armed D. L. Bonney, and Clint had returned the borrowed gun and allowed the three of them to leave. When he asked the bartender for two beers the man had announced they were "on the house."

"These people think I'm some sort of monster," Bonney complained.

"Next time," Clint said, "I'll leave you alone and let you take a beating."

"Oh," Bonney said, "they wouldn't have hurt me."

"They would have pounded you into the floor," Clint said, "and then stepped over you and not given you a second thought."

"I can't believe that," Bonney said. "You always say I have no sense of humor. I just thought they were, you know, kidding."

"They weren't," Clint said. "When you left the restaurant I told you to watch out for yourself."

"I didn't do anything wrong."

"D. L.," Clint said, "I've got to tell you something."

"What?"

"I'm finding it harder and harder to believe that you're a newspaperman."

"Why?"

"Well . . . you're kind of naive, don't you think?"

"No," Bonney said, "I just think I'm a little out of my element here."

"A little?" Clint asked. "I'm surprised you survived until you met up with me."

"Well, how was I to know you had so many unreason-able people out here?"

"See?" Clint said. "That's what I mean."

"What?"

"I've been back East many times, D. L.," Clint said. "There are these kinds of people all over. How could you not know that?"

Bonney looked away and said, "Well, I guess I just haven't run into them yet."

"Come on," Clint said, "fess up. How much writing have you actually done for newspapers? What are you really doing out here?"

Bonney stared into his beer mug for a while before answering.

"Okay," he said, "so I haven't actually had a lot of stuff published in the newspapers. I have been writing, though."

"Have you had anything published?"

"Um, well, some, um, letters."

"Do you know anyone in the newspaper business?"

"Actually, I have an uncle who owns a paper in Chi-cago."

"Have you gone to him?"

"No."

"Why not?"

"I'm not looking for a handout."

"So what's out here for you?"

"That much was true," he said. "I'm looking for Han-son to write about him. When I've done that then I can go to my uncle and see if he'll print it."

"Is he your mother's brother?"

"Yes, but she can't help. She's dead."

"I see," Clint said. "What kind of a relationship do you have with him?"

Bonney made a face.

"Not much. I'm just hoping that my writing will catch his eye."

"You took journalism in college?"

"Yes."

"How old are you?"

"Twenty-four," he said.

Clint looked surprised.

"I know," Bonney said, "I look older."

"If you'd said thirty I wouldn't have been surprised."

"When I'm thirty," he said, "I'll look forty. I can't help it."

"How's your money holding up?" Clint asked. "I've been wondering about that, too. I thought your expenses were being paid."

"Well, they're not," he said. "I had a small inheritance when my mother died. I've used most of it for this trip."

"How much longer can you last?"

"Not much," he admitted.

"If you run out of money how are you going to get back home?"

"Where's home?" Bonney asked.

"Chicago?"

"No, that's where my uncle is," he said. "I really don't have anyplace to go to. If my uncle is impressed, then I'd go to Chicago. If he's not . . ." Bonney shrugged. "It won't matter where I am."

Clint studied Bonney a lot closer than he had before. The naive outlook was explained a bit by the fact that he was only twenty-four. Studying him now he could see the youth in his eyes. He had a high forehead, which contributed to the fact that he looked older than he was.

"Maybe this fella Waterstone will be able to tell us something," Clint said.

"I hope so," Bonney said. "Now that you know I'm

a fake I guess I can confess to being worried about money and all.''

''You're not a fake, D. L.—is that really your name?''

Bonney laughed.

''That much is true.''

''Well,'' Clint said, ''I don't think of you as a fake. In fact, I think you showed a lot of courage by coming out west this way.''

''Really?''

''Yes,'' Clint said. ''I just question your choice of subject.''

''You think I should write about you?''

''No,'' Clint said, ''not about me, but there's a lot to write about out here—that is, if your Hanson story doesn't turn out.''

''Do you think I should give up on Hanson?''

''No,'' Clint said, ''you came this far, I think you should see it through. Besides, *I* want to see it through now.''

Bonney nodded.

''I guess I should stick with you then,'' he said, ''or I might get killed.''

''It looks like we'll have to talk to Waterstone tomorrow,'' Clint said. ''After that we'll decide what we're going to do.''

At that moment a man came through the batwing doors, and Clint noticed he was wearing a badge.

''Looks like we're about to be visited by the local law.''

''Why?'' Bonney asked. ''Because of what happened?''

''Maybe,'' Clint said, ''or maybe he just wants to check on the strangers who rode into town. Just sit back, relax, and let me do the talking, okay?''

Bonney sat back and said, ''With pleasure.''

THIRTY-ONE

Clint watched the sheriff as he scanned the room, and took the time to study the man. He was tall, broad through the shoulders, looked at this distance to be in his late thirties—but learning that Bonney was only twenty-four kept him from making a snap judgment about age. The man was rugged-looking, though, and appeared to be physically up to the job of upholding the law.

Finally, the man's eyes fell on him and Bonney, and he started toward them.

"Here he comes. . . ."

The man stopped at their table and looked down at them. He was taller than Clint had first realized, and older.

"You gents just get to town today?" he asked.

"That's right, Sheriff."

The sheriff looked at Bonney.

"I understand you're hell with a gun."

"Huh?" Bonney didn't know what to say.

"I'm afraid that was my little joke, Sheriff."

"A joke?"

"Seems my friend here was being picked on by three of your citizens, made fun of because he wasn't wearing a gun. I took it upon myself to, uh, tell a little story."

"I see," the man said, then looked at Bonney again. "Well, I didn't think you looked like hell with a gun."

"Thanks," Bonney said, "I guess."

"But you," the sheriff said, switching his gaze to Clint, "look like you can handle yourself. You mind telling me your name?"

"No, Sheriff," Clint said, "I don't mind at all. My name's Clint Adams."

The sheriff stared at him for a few moments, then nodded his head.

"Well, I guess that explains things," the man said. "My name's Ritter, I've been sheriff here for about five years. We're, uh, not used to having famous people hereabouts."

Clint ignored the "famous people" remark.

"My friend here is D. L. Bonney. He's a writer from back East, came out here to write about the West. I'm afraid your friends gave him the wrong impression about us."

"They're not my friends," the lawman said, "just some hands from the Waterstone ranch who came into town for some fun. Seems like they picked on the wrong men."

"They work for Waterstone?"

"Do you know him?"

"No, but we came here to talk to him."

"Oh? What about?"

"We have a friend in common."

"Who would that be?"

"His name's Rick Hartman."

"I don't know him," the lawman said after a moment.

"No reason why you should."

"I guess you'll be going out to the ranch tomorrow?"

"That's right."

"Well," the sheriff said, "try to stay out of trouble the rest of tonight, will you?"

"It's always my aim to stay out of trouble, Sheriff," Clint explained. "You seem to have a nice, quiet town. I don't want to do anything to change that."

"I'm glad to hear that, Mr. Adams," the sheriff said. He looked at Bonney and said, "I hope you find some good things to write about."

"I'm sure I will."

The sheriff nodded, turned, and walked out.

"It's amazing," Bonney said.

"What is?"

"The deference with which you're treated when people find out who you are."

"I prefer to think of it as respect," Clint said.

"Or is it fear?" Bonney asked.

"I guess," Clint said, "it's a little of all three, huh?"

"I guess so."

"Well," Clint said, "word will get around now that you're not some kind of heller with a gun. That should make you feel better."

"But word will get around about who you are, too."

"Yes, it will."

"Is that likely to cause trouble?"

"I don't rightly know, D. L.," Clint said. "Listen, I've got a date to walk a lady home. Why don't you go back to the hotel?"

"Good idea," Bonney said. "With word getting around that I'm not a gunman I think that would be a safe place for me."

"I think I agree," Clint said.

THIRTY-TWO

Clint made sure that Bonney got back to the hotel all right and then went on to the restaurant to walk Gloria home. He didn't know how the three ranch hands would react when they realized they'd been made fools of. The hotel was definitely the place for Bonney to be.

When Clint reached the restaurant Gloria was standing outside, waiting.

"I hope you haven't been waiting long," he said.

"Five minutes," she said. "It's all right."

"Which way do we go?"

"This way," she said.

They started walking toward the south end of town.

"I have a house," she said. "My husband and I bought it, and then he died—I mean, that close. He died a week after we moved in."

"How did he die?"

122

"Well . . . he was killed. He was the sheriff at the time."

"That was before Sheriff Ritter."

"Yes, it was," she said. "Cal Ritter was my husband's deputy."

"I see."

"We were going to fill this house with children, and now I live there alone."

Clint was starting to regret that he'd asked her to let him walk her home. She was a nice woman, but he wasn't looking to get to know her quite *this* well.

"It must be hard maintaining the house on what you make as a waitress."

"Not at all," she said. "Since my husband—his name was Ralph—since Ralph was killed while he was sheriff, the town decided to give me the house, free and clear."

"I'm sure that didn't make up for your loss."

"I've tried to sell the damned thing since then," she said, "but nobody wants it."

"What would you do with the money if you did sell it?"

"I'd leave here," she said, "move someplace else and start over."

"Move where?"

"Someplace exciting," she said. "Denver, maybe San Francisco. Someplace where there's a lot of people."

"Weatherby looks like a nice little town."

"It is," she said, "but there are just too many damned reminders of what my life was going to be like."

When they reached the house Clint saw what she meant about filling it with children. It was a two-story house that was just too big for her.

They stopped at the door and she asked, "Would you like to come in?"

"I don't think so, Gloria," he said. "It probably wouldn't be a good idea."

"I've scared you, haven't I?"

"Well—"

"What if I told you there would be no strings attached?" she said. "That it would just be one night?"

"I, uh, do you mean—"

"What if I said I just wanted to sleep with a man again?" she said. "That it had been a long time since a man held me, or since I'd met a man I wanted to hold me?"

"Gloria—"

"Should I say please, Clint?" she asked. "Should I beg?"

He regarded her for a moment, then said, "No, Gloria. A woman as lovely as you shouldn't have to beg, not for any man to hold her."

"Good," she said. "Then you'll come in."

"Yes."

"And just so there are no misunderstandings," she said, "it's just for one night."

"Yes."

"I don't want you to marry me or take me with you when you leave town."

"All right."

She put the key into the lock, opened the door, and he followed her in.

Sheriff Cal Ritter followed Clint Adams and Gloria Manning from the restaurant where she worked to her house. He watched as they stopped in front of the house and talked awhile, and then while she unlocked the door and they both went in. He watched, and his heart ached to see her take a man into her house with her, a stranger like Clint Adams.

Even while he had been Ralph Manning's deputy, Cal Ritter had been in love with Gloria Manning. After Ralph was killed and he was appointed Sheriff, he had waited a respectable time before asking her to marry him. He had just won reelection and thought it was a good time to propose. Her reaction had surprised him. She'd said no, that she didn't want to be married to another man who wore a badge. Then when he told her that he would give up the badge, she told him that she didn't love him.

That was when he told her that he'd wait—he'd wait until she *did* love him, and then he'd take off his badge and marry her.

He'd been waiting years now. She had not been with another man during all that time, and he'd felt that they were getting closer and closer to the time when they would marry.

But now, after all this time, this stranger had come to town and she had taken him into her house with her. If she just wanted to be with a man, why not him? Why Clint Adams? A man who would take her and then leave town, leaving her behind. Did she think that he'd take her with him? Could she be that gullible?

Adams had probably sweet-talked her. Here Ritter had been waiting patiently, not pressing her, and Clint Adams came to town and sweet-talked his way right into her bed the first day.

He was disappointed in her. That was the behavior of a slut, not a respectable woman.

Ritter stood staring at the house long enough to see a light go on inside, and then go out shortly thereafter. It pained him to think of Gloria in bed with Clint Adams, the bed she'd shared with her husband, and the bed Ritter hoped she would share with him someday.

Now that hope was gone.

Clint Adams had come to Weatherby and shattered

everything Cal Ritter had been working toward. He'd
turned Gloria Manning into a slut, and in the morning
he'd be on his way, not caring about the damage he was
leaving behind.

Well, if that's what he thought he was going to do, he
was in for a big surprise.

THIRTY-THREE

"I should have bathed," Gloria said.

"Hush," he said, even though she smelled like cooking. Her mouth was sweet, though, when he kissed her, and when he undressed her, her body was warm and soft and full, a woman's body, built for the giving and receiving of pleasure.

The first time he entered her she was lying on her back, her legs tightly around him.

"God," she hissed from between clenched teeth, "it's been so long. Slow, go slow . . ."

He went slow, moving in and out of her, kissing her mouth and her neck, her breasts and nipples. He continued to move slowly until finally she urged him to move faster, to take her harder. She gasped when her time came and he felt her shudder, and then she gasped again when he exploded inside of her. . . .

• • •

By this time the three men were outside the house, watching and waiting. They didn't care how long it took, even if they had to stay there until morning. No one made fools of them the way this man did and got away with it.

No one, no matter who he was.

Each man was armed with a pistol and a rifle, because of who the man was. They weren't going to take any chances, not with this man.

They were well armed, and patient. . . .

The second time he entered her she was on top, her breasts dangling before his face so that he could lift his head and kiss them. He held them together at one point and actually sucked both nipples at the same time. She caught her breath and continued to move up and down on his rigid shaft.

"This one night," she had told him during the in-between time, "has to make up for a long time of doing without."

"I'm here," he'd said. "Use me. . . ."

And she was. She pressed her hands down on his sternum while she continued to hump up and down on him. Her eyes were closed, and he thought that a gunfight could have broken out in the room and she wouldn't have noticed. He was amazed at how much pleasure he was getting just from watching her. She was like a woman who had just discovered sex—or, more to the point, had rediscovered it.

"Ooooh." It was a long, guttural sound, one of pure pleasure, and hearing it excited him more. He began to lift his butt off the bed to meet her thrusts, and soon they were grunting and groaning together, straining toward one another, sweating and moaning, the sound of their flesh meeting making slapping sounds in the room.

Finally she brought herself down on him and stayed

there, grinding herself against him while waves of pleasure overtook her. When he exploded this time he didn't know who shouted the loudest, him or her. . . .

"God," she said, "it was nothing like I remembered."

"Like you said," he answered, "it's been a long time."

"No, you don't understand," she said. "I remember what it was like to have sex with my husband, and it was nothing like . . . this."

"Are you sad?"

"God, no!" she said, laughing. "How could I be sad about this? It was wonderful."

"I thought . . ."

"No," she said. "I loved my husband, Clint, but the fact of the matter is he didn't . . . like sex all that much. His mother was very strict and brought him up to believe that sex was something sinful and bad. She taught him that men and women only did it to have children, and if they enjoyed it, it was a sin."

"That's a shame," Clint said. "You and he could have enjoyed each other much more than you did."

"Yes," she said, "yes, we could have."

"Do you hear from his mother anymore?"

"She died," Gloria said. "I have no living relatives, his or mine."

"It must be lonely."

"I have friends," she said, resting her head on his shoulder, "but yes, it does get lonely, sometimes."

"What about men?" he asked. "You must have had . . . suitors since your husband's death."

"One," she said, "and his being there scared other men away."

"Oh? Who is it?"

"Cal Ritter."

"The sheriff?"

She nodded.

"He wants to marry me. He's asked me many times."

"And why won't you?"

"Simple," she said. "I don't love him. I'm not even attracted to him, but he insists that the day will come when we'll marry. Any other man who shows interest in me quickly gets scared away."

She put her hand on his chest and raised her head so she could look at him.

"You've shown more than an interest," she said, "and I've shown it back. If I were you, I'd be careful."

"I'm always careful."

"I guess I should have told you before. . . ."

"It wouldn't have made a difference," he assured her.

"No," she said, putting her head back down on his shoulder, "I don't think it would have. Do you have to leave?"

"No."

"Good," she said. "We can rest a bit, and then try again."

"Sure . . ." he started to say, but suddenly became aware of the fact that she had fallen asleep.

THIRTY-FOUR

They made love one more time and then Clint left, telling Gloria that she needed her sleep if she was going to work tomorrow. She said damn it, she did have to work, and why had she found a man who was so sensible?

Clint kissed her good night and left her snuggled under the covers of her bed, all warm and comfortable and smelling of sex.

It was very hard to leave, but he managed it.

"Hey!"

Sid Parks nudged both of his dozing partners, Eli Louis and Dale Smith.

"Wha—" Smith said.

"It's him," Parks said, "he's comin' out."

"'Bout time," Smith muttered.

They both shook Louis until he was awake. By this

131

time Clint Adams was in the street, walking back toward the center of town.

"How do we do this?" Parks asked.

"I can get him from here," Louis said.

"Don't be stupid," Smith snapped. "He's got to know it's us, and he's got to know why."

"So what do we do?" Parks asked.

"Let's take the back way to his hotel," Smith suggested. "We'll catch him in a cross fire. Come on, I'll explain on the way."

As Clint approached his hotel he knew something was wrong. It was his sixth sense, which he had come to heed so well over the years.

He stopped, still well off from the hotel, and stared into the darkness.

Someone was waiting for him. He was sure of this. Could it have been Ritter, the sheriff? Going to try and scare him away from Gloria? Or somebody else, someone who recognized him and wanted to try his luck?

He decided to stand still and wait.

"What's he waitin' for?" Parks hissed.

"Quiet!" Smith called back.

"What?" Louis called.

"Shut up, both of you!" Smith whispered loudly, but it was too late.

"Come on out!" Clint called. "We can do this in the street."

No answer.

"I'm not coming near the hotel," Clint said, "so you might as well come out."

He waited and then, one by one, they came out of hiding. One on the left side of the entrance, and two from the right. He recognized them immediately. The three men from the saloon.

"Oh, it's you."

"You made fools of us with your phony story about your friend," Smith said.

"It was all in fun."

"We don't like bein' made fun of," Smith said.

"Uh, no, we don't," said Louis, when Smith nudged him hard.

"So what do you intend to do now?" Clint asked. "Make fools of yourselves again, only this time where nobody can see?"

"You got to learn," Parks said.

"Learn what?"

There was a pause, as if they didn't know who was supposed to talk next.

"Not to make fools of people."

"Okay," Clint said, "let's consider that I've learned that lesson. Why don't you boys go home?"

"You got to learn to leave our women alone, too."

Smith nudged Louis, hard.

"Why'd you say that?" he hissed.

Clint frowned. If they knew about Gloria they must have followed him from her house—only how had they known?

Ritter. Had the sheriff sent them after him? He'd find out about that later.

"This is your call, boys," Clint said.

There was a bright moon out, so they could see each other clearly.

Two of the men, Louis and Parks, looked at the other— Smith. Obviously, it was his call, and they'd go along with it.

"Watch him, boys," Clint said to them. "Your friend is going to get you killed."

"Don't listen to him," Smith said, "he's only one man."

"That may be," Clint said, "but you boys are holding rifles. Rifles are bad news this close up. You'd have to drop them and go for your pistols, and I don't have that problem."

He let that sink in and then said, "If one of you makes a wrong move, I'll kill all three of you."

He saw at least one of the men stiffen, which meant he was going to hesitate. He'd kill the leader first, then the second man, and worry about that man last.

"Come on, come on," Clint said, "I need my sleep. If you're going to do it, do it now!"

Abruptly, that third man threw his rifle to the ground and raised his hands.

"Wait! Wait! Don't do it."

"Goddamn it!" Smith shouted at Parks, the man who had dropped his rifle.

"We can't do it just the two of us, Dale," Louis said.

"Shit, shit!" Smith said.

"Drop your guns."

Parks took out his pistol and tossed it to the ground.

"You're gonna pay for this, Parks," Smith said, dropping his rifle.

"Least I'll be alive to pay for it," the man said.

Louis also dropped his rifle.

"You two, take out your pistols with your left hands and drop them."

Louis and Smith did as they were told.

"Now move along. You can pick up your guns tomorrow."

"From where?" Smith asked. "The sheriff?"

"No," Clint said, "I'll leave them someplace, and I'll leave word with the clerk at the hotel."

"Let's get out of here, Dale," Louis said.

Parks was already walking away, his hands still in the air.

"You ain't heard the last of this," Smith said, pointing his finger at Clint.

"You tell Sheriff Ritter to do his own dirty work next time, boys."

"How did you—" Louis started.

"Shut up and get moving!" Smith said.

Clint watched them closely as they walked away, then moved in and scooped up all their guns. When he walked into the hotel carrying them the clerk's eyes widened.

"Is there a problem?" he asked.

"No problem."

Clint deposited the guns on the desk.

"Shall I call the sheriff?"

"No," Clint said, "I just want you to put these in one of your bathtubs. You, uh, do have bath facilities here, don't you?"

"Yessir."

"Well, put these in there overnight," Clint said.

"Er . . . and then what?"

"We'll talk about that in the morning," Clint said. "Good night."

"Good night, sir."

The clerk watched Clint walk upstairs, then stared at the guns awhile before picking them up off the desk.

THIRTY-FIVE

In the morning, at breakfast in the hotel dining room, Clint told Bonney what had happened in the street in front of the hotel.

"My God!" Bonney said. "You could have been killed while I slept."

"Judging by what I heard last night passing your door," Clint said. "I doubt that you were sleeping."

Walking past Bonney's door Clint had heard a woman moaning and crying out.

"Well," Bonney said, looking away, "I was in bed . . . and you could have been killed."

"Not by those boys," Clint said. "I talked them out of it once, I figured I could do it again. What I'm concerned with is who sent them."

"Why did anyone have to send them? Maybe they were just mad at you."

136

"No," Clint said, "I think they were pushed into it. They knew where I was. They must have been watching the house."

"How could anyone know that you'd end up in the waitress's house?"

"I think the sheriff knew."

Bonney gaped.

"You think the sheriff sent them after you?"

Clint nodded.

"Why?"

"He's in love with Gloria."

Bonney gave him a blank look.

"The waitress."

"But he's the sheriff."

"And they don't do things like that?" Clint asked.

"Well . . . you wouldn't think so."

"I should find your faith in human nature encouraging," Clint said, "but I'm afraid it will get you killed someday."

"Well, what do we do now?"

"We finish breakfast," Clint said, "and then we go out and see Sam Waterstone. Maybe after that we can just leave town. That should make everybody happy."

They continued to eat in silence until Bonney asked, "How was she?"

"What?"

"Gloria, the waitress," Bonney said. "How was she?"

"I don't usually talk about it afterward, D. L.," Clint said.

There was another moment of silence and then Bonney asked, "Do you want to hear about the girl I was with?"

"No!" Clint said. "Just eat."

Cal Ritter sat in his office, waiting. He hadn't heard from Smith, Parks, and Louis, but he hadn't heard any shooting last night. Also, no one was reporting any dead bodies. Obviously, the men had not been able to accomplish anything against Clint Adams. Most likely Adams had scared them out of it.

So where was Adams this morning? Surely he must have learned from one of the three men that Ritter had prodded them into going after him. Why was he not here confronting him?

Ritter actually regretted sending the men after him. It had been a stupid reaction to seeing Adams and Gloria go into her house. Even if something happened between them, Clint Adams was not about to stay in Weatherby. With any luck he'd be on his way today, after he talked to Sam Waterstone. All Ritter had had to do was leave the situation alone and it would have resolved itself through Adams's departure.

Now he had to sit and wait for the man to come after him, and then play dumb when he was confronted. Surely, he would say, those three men were just looking to blame someone else for their stupidity—while Ritter, of course, was looking to hide his.

THIRTY-SIX

They walked to the livery to reclaim their horses, which had been well cared for.

"Leaving town?" the liveryman asked.

"We're not sure," Clint said. Actually, they had not checked out of the hotel.

"Well, just bring 'em on back if you come back," the man said. "That big black is something special."

"Yes," Clint said, patting Duke's neck, "he is."

They left Weatherby and rode out to the Waterstone ranch. As they approached the house they drove through an iron gate that bore the brand WAS, which stood—obviously—for Waterstone.

As they rode up to the house several men were around, and one in particular stepped forward to meet them. He was tall and young, maybe a couple of years older than D. L. Bonney.

"Can I help you?"

"We'd like to see Mr. Waterstone," Clint said.

"Which one?"

"How many are there?"

The young man laughed.

"I'm Charlie Waterstone. I'm the foreman. My father is Sam. He owns the place."

"It's Sam that we want to see, then."

"What's it about?"

"Well, in a way, the Tappia brothers."

Charlie Waterstone made a face.

"Those losers? Are they friends of yours?"

"No, they're not. We don't even know them."

"Who are you?"

"This is D. L. Bonney, a writer from back East," Clint said. "My name is Clint Adams."

"Adams . . ." Waterstone said.

"That's right."

Bonney was still fascinated by the reactions of people when they found out who Clint was.

"Would you tell your father that we're here to see him?" Clint asked.

"Uh, sure," Charlie Waterstone said. "Wait right here."

Waterstone walked to the front door of the house, which was just one step up, and entered. The house was big, but not extremely large. Clint had expected something ostentatious, not unassuming.

"Let's dismount," Clint said.

"How do we know he'll even see us?" Bonney asked.

"He'll see us," Clint said. "If I know Rick, he sent a telegram."

The front door of the house opened and Charlie Waterstone came out. Now that he wasn't on horseback Clint could see that the man was tall, perhaps six two or three. He waved and a couple of men came running over.

"Give your horses to them," he said. "They'll be well cared for. I'll take you in to see my father."

"Be careful," Clint said, handing one of the men Duke's reins, "he'll take a finger if he doesn't like you."

"Thanks," the man said, "I'll be careful."

"Gentlemen," Charlie said, "this way."

They followed him into the house. The inside was un-cluttered by interior walls. To the left was a dining room, to the right a living room, with no walls to block them off. It was all one space.

"This is very nice," Clint said, "airy. I like it."

"There's a kitchen back there," Charlie said, pointing beyond the dining room, "and my father's den is in there." He pointed to a closed door off the living room. "He'll be out in a minute."

Clint looked around and didn't see a woman's hand anywhere. It was a distinctly masculine house.

"No women," Charlie said.

"What?"

"I know what you're thinking," he said. "My mother died ten years ago, and the cook is a man. You were thinking there's no woman's touch here."

"That's right."

"After she died," Charlie said, "my mother, that is, my father changed the whole house over. He misses her."

"I would think he'd want to keep something of her around," Bonney said.

Charlie Waterstone looked at Bonney.

"He says he doesn't need anything to remind him of her."

"I see," Bonney said and vowed to remain silent on the subject the rest of the time they were there.

"Can I get you something to drink?" Charlie asked.

"No, thanks," Clint said.

The younger Waterstone took off his hat, revealing a

shock of jet-black hair. He tossed the hat aside. He wasn't wearing a gun, but then why would he while he was on his own land?

"Can you give me some idea what this is about?" he asked.

"Um, to tell the truth, it's kind of hard to explain. I think I'd rather wait for your father to come out, and then I can try explaining it to both of you."

"Fair enough."

At that moment the door to Sam Waterstone's den opened and one of the largest men Clint had ever seen filled the doorway. Charlie Waterstone had his father's height, but none of his girth. Clint was surprised that he fit through the doorway, and then when he did he seemed to fill the room. He had the same shock of hair his son did, but his was snow-white, as was his beard.

"Gentlemen," he said, "I'm Sam Waterstone. Welcome to my home."

THIRTY-SEVEN

Clint made the introductions and they shook hands with the big man.

"Did you offer our guests something to drink?" Waterstone asked.

"Yes, Pa—"

"He did," Clint said. "We're fine."

"Well, come in and sit down."

They moved into the living room portion of the house, and Waterstone lowered himself into an overstuffed chair that looked like it had taken a beating for years. Clint assumed it was the man's private chair. He and Bonney sat on the sofa, which appeared barely used.

"I got a telegram from Rick Hartman about you, Mr. Adams," Waterstone said. "He didn't mention Mr. Bonney."

"Rick doesn't know Mr. Bonney," Clint said.

"Well, I barely know Mr. Hartman, myself," Sam Waterstone said. "I simply remember him as a good, honest businessman."

"Well, he is that."

"I have to admit I'm very curious about why the Gunsmith would be coming to see me."

"It's a little complicated," Clint said, "but I'll try to simplify it. You see, we're looking for a man named Hanson."

"Wild Bull Hanson?" Waterstone asked.

"Yes," Clint said. "Do you know him?"

Waterstone exchanged a glance with his son.

"I know of him," Waterstone said. "In fact, we received a telegram about him as well as you."

"Really?" Clint asked. "Would that have been from the Tappia brothers?"

"Jimmy Tappia, yes," the elder Waterstone said.

"They mentioned the Tappia brothers outside, Pa," Charlie Waterstone said, "but they say they don't know them."

"Do you?"

"No, sir, we don't," Clint said.

"Then how do you know of them?" Waterstone said. "Surely they haven't gone and gotten themselves a reputation I don't know about?"

"Not that I know of," Clint said. "You see, we came across their name while looking for Hanson . . ."

He proceeded to tell the Waterstones what they found when they reached the town of Zackel, Colorado.

"You mean those idiots killed a woman?" Waterstone asked.

"Apparently one of them did," Clint said, "but the sheriff can't prove it."

"I knew they were stupid," Waterstone said, "but I didn't know they were that stupid."

"I did," Charlie Waterstone said.

"If I may ask," Clint said, "what's your connection with them?"

"With them?" Waterstone said. "None. Their father, he was my friend, my good friend. That's why I've tried not to think too harshly of them."

"They're nothing like their father was," Charlie said. "Even I know that, and I only barely remember him."

"Are they your age?" Clint asked.

"One of them yes, the others are older."

"One of them, Bobby," Waterstone said, "he was killed four months ago."

"Do you know by whom?" Clint asked.

"No—wait," Waterstone said. "I understand now. You think he was killed by this Hanson?"

"I think *they* think he was."

"And you're looking for Hanson."

"Right."

"So you think if you find the Tappias, you'll find Hanson."

"Right."

Waterstone spread his arms magnanimously.

"That's not so hard to understand."

"Good," Clint said. "Mr. Waterstone—"

"Call me Sam."

"Sam, you said you got a telegram from Jimmy Tappia?"

"That's right," Waterstone said. "He's calling in all of his father's markers, trying to find this Hanson."

"And do you know where Hanson is?"

Waterstone did not answer right away.

"Pa?"

He looked at his son.

"Tell 'em."

"I think I know where Hanson is," Sam Waterstone said.

"Where?" Bonney asked.

"Have you told the Tappias?"

"No, I haven't," Waterstone said, "not yet."

"Why not?"

"I got their telegram about the time I got Rick Hartman's," the man said. "I guess I just wanted to hear what you had to say."

"You suspected that the two were related?" Clint asked.

"Yes."

"Coincidence," Bonney said, without looking at Clint.

"Yes."

"Sam, will you tell us where Hanson is?"

The older Waterstone looked at the younger, who nodded.

"I have an idea, but I can't be sure."

"Can you make sure?"

Waterstone nodded.

"I can send a telegram and find out."

"We'll have to go into town—"

"That's not a problem," Waterstone said.

"Uh, I may have a problem in town," Clint said.

"What problem?"

Clint told the Waterstones what had happened last night, right up to the jealous sheriff. He didn't say whether or not the sheriff had a reason to be jealous.

"I'll go to town, too," Charlie said.

"I'll talk to the sheriff," Sam said. "He won't be a problem. Just let me get ready."

"I'll get the buckboard," Charlie said.

Sam looked sheepishly at Clint.

"I'm afraid I've outgrown horseback riding."

Clint didn't say anything to that. He didn't know what to say, except, "Thank you for your help."

"If those Tappia boys killed a woman," Sam said, "I want to see them get what's coming to them."

THIRTY-EIGHT

Charlie Waterstone brought his father's buckboard around, along with his own horse, a healthy-looking roan.

"We tried a buggy," he said, somewhat embarrassed, "but he outgrew that, too."

They were waiting for Sam to come out.

"How much does he weigh?" Bonney asked.

Clint had thought about the question but had decided not to ask. D. L. Bonney did not have that tact, but Charlie didn't seem to mind.

"We're not sure anymore," he said. "We figure he must be close to four hundred pounds by now."

"Was he always . . . big?" Clint asked.

"He was always a big man, yes, but he only started getting fat ten years ago . . . after Ma died. He hasn't gone out much since then."

The front door opened and Sam Waterstone came out, squinting at the sun. Some of the ranch hands had stopped

what they were doing to look. Clint guessed that it had
been a long time since they'd actually seen their boss.

Charlie had to help his father into the buckboard, but
once he was in the seat the older man drove it himself.

"Let's go," he said.

Duke and Bonney's horse had been brought around also
and now the two men and Charlie Waterstone mounted
up and followed behind the buckboard to town.

When they pulled up to the livery stable the liveryman
came out.

"Mr. Waterstone!" he called out. "It's been a while."

"Hello, Joe," Waterstone said. "You want to take care
of the rig and team for me? And these other horses?"

"Sure, Mr. Waterstone, sure."

They all watched while Charlie helped his father down
from the buckboard. Once his feet were on the ground
Sam seemed to move around pretty well.

"Let's go see the sheriff first," Sam said, "and then
we'll go to the telegraph office."

"Sure, Pa," Charlie said.

Clint and Bonney were willing to tag along, if it got
them what they wanted.

Outside the sheriff's office Sam said to Charlie, Clint,
and Bonney, "I'll go in and talk to Cal. He'll listen to
me. You boys just wait out here."

Charlie looked at Clint, who nodded.

"Sure, Pa."

Sam nodded and went into the office.

"Will the sheriff listen to your father?" Bonney asked.

"He will if he wants to keep his job," Charlie said.
"Cal's afraid of Pa."

"I thought he was voted into office," Bonney said,
frowning.

"He was," Charlie said, "by my pa."

"By one man?" Bonney asked.

"There's something to write about," Clint said.

Before Bonney could say anything the door opened and Sam Waterstone came out. Clint was again struck by just how big the man really was.

"You won't have any more trouble in Weatherby," he said to Clint.

"Just like that?" Bonney asked.

"Yeah," Sam said, "just like that. Come on, telegraph office next."

They followed behind and Clint wondered how a man who weighed so much could walk so fast that the three of them had to trot to keep up.

THIRTY-NINE

Sam Waterstone came out of the telegraph office, waving a reply.

"You got that right away?" Clint asked.

"People respond to Pa," Charlie said proudly.

"This," Waterstone said, handing Clint the telegram, "is where Bull Hanson is headed."

"Where he's headed?" Bonney asked. "Not where he is?"

"I could tell you where he is," Sam said, "but by the time you got there, he'd be gone. This way you know where he's headed, and you can get there while he's still there, or even before him."

"How did you get this?" Clint asked.

"Contacts."

"Pa's got a lot of contacts," Charlie said proudly.

Clint thought he had a lot of contacts, too, but appar-

ently he didn't have as many—or as many *good* ones—
as Sam Waterstone.

He looked at the telegram, which had the name GAR-
RETT on it.

"Is this the name of a town?"

Sam nodded.

"It's right on the border of Kansas, north of here about
two days' ride."

"And he's headed there."

"That's my information," Sam said. "He was in a
town called Tylerville, but now he's headed for Garrett.
If you start now, you might beat him there."

"And what about the Tappia brothers?" Clint asked.
"Are you going to give them this information?"

Sam pulled at his lower lip for a few moments.

"I don't know if Hanson killed their brother or not,"
he said finally, "but out of respect for their father I think
I have to give them this information."

"I understand," Clint said, although he wasn't sure he
did. The man Sam had respect for was dead, and the three
surviving sons were, by all accounts, lazy, shiftless, and—
according to the sheriff of Zackel—at least one of them
was a killer.

"Can I ask a favor?"

"Sure, go ahead," Sam said, as if Clint hadn't already
asked for enough.

"Could you hold off a day before giving them the information?"

"Sure," Sam said. "It might take me that long to get
it to them anyway."

"I appreciate it."

"Can I ask you something?"

"Sure."

"What's your business with this Hanson fella?"

"Well," Clint said, "D. L., here, wants to write about him."

"If everything I've heard about him is true," Bonney added.

"And you?" Sam asked Clint.

"My reasons are more personal," Clint said.

"I won't ask, then."

"No, it's okay," Clint replied. "I don't like him using the name Wild Bull. I feel he's trying to trade on the reputation of a deceased friend of mine."

Sam nodded and said, "You mean Hickok?"

Clint nodded.

"I can see your point," Sam said. "You and Hickok were good friends, weren't you?"

"He was my best friend."

"Is there anything else I can do for you?" Sam asked. "I could send some men with you."

"No, that's not necessary."

"How about Charlie, here?" Sam asked, clapping his son on the shoulder.

"No," Clint said, "he's your foreman, you need him here. We don't need any men, Sam, we're not looking for any trouble."

"Mixing you in with Hanson and the Tappia boys," Sam said, "that sounds like a formula for trouble to me, Clint. Are you sure?"

"Positive."

"When are you leaving?" Sam asked. "Can I offer you the hospitality of my table and my house?"

"You've done enough for us as it is, Sam," Clint said. "I think we'll just start for Garrett today."

"Well, then, I wish you luck."

Sam extended his hand and Clint shook it, then Charlie's, and then Bonney did the same.

"Charlie, we got some errands we can take care of while we're in town, don't we?"

"Yes, Pa."

The Waterstones went off to tend to their errands, and Clint and Bonney walked back to their horses.

"He's an impressive man," Bonney said.

"Might even be somebody to write about, huh?" Clint asked.

"I was thinking that," Bonney said, as they mounted up. "I've been thinking about a lot of things."

"Like what?"

"Like there are a lot of better things I could write about than Wild Bull Hanson's reputation."

"You want to give up on him?"

"No," Bonney said, "I think I should see it through, at least talk to him. What about you?"

"Me?" Clint asked. "I'm going to Garrett, plain and simple."

"Okay, then," Bonney said, "let's go to Garrett and get this over with."

FORTY

Clint and Bonney rode into Garrett almost forty-eight hours from the time they left Weatherby. Garrett appeared to be a typical town, neither on the rise nor the decline. It was probably a town that was happy with itself the way it was.

"We made damn good time," Bonney said, proud of himself for being able to ride for two days without complaining. "Do you think we beat him here?"

"I don't know," Clint said, "but I guess we'll find out soon enough."

He tried talking to the liveryman when they gave over their horses for care.

"Seems like a quiet town."

"Yup." The man was tight-lipped, a practice he'd probably learned over his sixty-odd years was advisable.

"Get many strangers?"

"Nope."

"Guess we're the first ones you've seen in a while then, huh?"

"Yup."

Clint looked at Bonney, who shrugged.

They left the livery to continue with the monotony.

"Doesn't it get to you sometimes?" Bonney asked. "I mean, with all the traveling you do? It seems like we've been going from livery stable to livery stable, from hotel to hotel."

"Usually," Clint said, "when I go someplace I stay awhile. We've been moving around pretty often because we're looking for someone."

"And maybe we'll finally find him."

They registered at the hotel, stowed their gear in their rooms, and made for the nearest saloon.

"The liveryman was kind of reluctant to talk," Clint said, "but I don't think we'll have that same problem with a bartender."

They entered the saloon, which was less than half full at that time of the afternoon. Given a few hours, though, that would change.

Clint decided to be more straightforward with the bartender, once they had their beers in their hands.

"Heard Bull Hanson was headed this way."

"Who?" The man seemed genuinely puzzled. He was tall, dark-haired, potbellied, and sweaty, and had probably been tending bar for twenty years or more. He had the look of a man who hadn't been out from behind the bar in years.

"Wild Bull Hanson?" Bonney said.

The man made a face.

"Don't know 'im," he said, "so if he was here, I wouldn't know it."

He moved away to take care of another thirsty customer.

"I'm confused," Bonney said.

"By what?"

"By the number of people who haven't heard of Hanson," he said. "Everybody seems to have heard of you."

"I've been around a little longer than Hanson."

"But how did his repute reach the East?"

"Maybe," Clint said, "by design."

"What do you mean?"

"I mean maybe he's lying in the places he thinks will do him some good."

"Lying?" Bonney asked. "Have you thought all along that his reputation is built on lies?"

"Most are, D. L."

"What about yours?"

"Not on any lies of mine," Clint said, "but certainly on the lies and exaggerations of others."

"And you have to live with it?"

Clint shrugged.

"That's the way it is, I'm afraid."

"Why don't you just . . . go away somewhere?"

"Oh, I've tried that before," Clint said. "It doesn't work. It all just catches up to you."

"I don't know how you can live like that."

"I don't have much choice."

After an awkward silence Bonney asked, "Uh, so what do we do now?"

"Now," Clint said, "I think we just have to wait. If our information is correct, somebody should be getting here pretty soon."

FORTY-ONE

After two days Clint and Bonney were beginning to wonder if Sam Waterstone's information was accurate.

"What if we read him wrong?" Bonney asked. "What if he really is friends with the Tappia brothers? What if he gave them the right information and sent us here?"

"I don't think that's the case," Clint said. "If he was wrong, that's one thing, but I don't think he was dishonest."

"How can you be sure?"

"I just don't think I read him wrong," Clint said. "I have confidence in my ability to read people."

"Well, I wish I did."

They were sitting in wooden chairs in front of the hotel, watching the street. Anyone coming into town would have to pass by them.

"I just don't think they're going to show up," Bonney said, "any of them."

"I think you're wrong."

"What makes you so—"

"Look."

Bonney, who had been looking at Clint, turned his head and looked at the street. He saw one man riding past them, wearing two guns and a well-trimmed beard and mustache.

"Jesus," Clint said, "he's even trying to look like Hickok."

"That's him?" Bonney asked. "That's Hanson?"

"That's him."

"How can you tell?"

"I can tell. Look at him. Even riding a horse he's strutting like a cock."

Bonney looked at Clint and was surprised by the expression on his face. His upper lip was curled, his teeth were bared, and he looked like he wanted to kill the man. His eyes followed the process of Bull Hanson as he continued to ride down the street.

"Clint?"

"Yeah?"

"What are you going to do?"

"Do?" Clint took his eyes off of Hanson, reluctantly, and looked at Bonney. "What do you think I'm going to do?"

"I don't know," Bonney said. "To tell you the truth, I'm afraid of what you're going to do."

"Well, I'm not going to do anything stupid, if that's what you're afraid of."

"Then wha—"

"Let him get settled," Clint said. "He might even come here to check in."

"And then what?"

"And then I'm going to talk to him," Clint said. "Just talk."

Bonney had seen Clint talk to men—like the three men in the saloon in Weatherby. Twice he talked them out of drawing their guns.

"When I'm finished with him," Clint continued, "you can have him."

Bonney frowned. When Clint was finished with him, would there be anything left?

During their first day in town Clint and Bonney had discussed the wisdom of going to the local law and announcing their presence.

"Normally," Clint had said, "I'd do it, but this is different."

"Why?"

"Once we tell him why we're here, and who we think is coming to town, he might order us to leave."

"And would we have to?"

Clint gave Bonney a look.

"If the local law tells you to leave, you're supposed to leave."

"But . . . he couldn't make you leave. Not you."

"Why not?"

"Well . . . because you're . . . you."

"I don't flaunt the law, D. L."

"Then if he told you to leave, you would?"

"Yes."

Bonney waited a moment, then said, "So . . . by not telling him you're here, you're not flaunting the law?"

"No."

"You're just sort of . . . circumventing it, for the moment."

"Yes."

Bonney wasn't sure he understood how *deceiving* the local lawman wasn't *flaunting* him, but he didn't question Clint on it.

• • •

But just because they hadn't talked to the local sheriff
didn't mean he hadn't noticed them. In fact, though, Sheriff Art Starr hadn't noticed Clint and Bonney until the
second day, yesterday, when they first took up their position in front of the hotel.

Starr had been sheriff of Garrett for twelve years, and
it was his opinion that he had stayed sheriff—and alive—
that long by being nonconfrontational. He did not auto-
matically assume that a stranger in town meant trouble,
and so he did not interview every stranger who came to
town. Instead he watched and waited, and if they caused
trouble—well, that was when he did his job.

Today he was in front of his office, watching Clint and
Bonney as they sat in front of the hotel, when the third
stranger rode into town.

Bull Hanson saw the two men sitting in front of the
hotel but did not acknowledge them. He knew they were
watching him, though, so they must have recognized him.
Good, his fame and his legend were spreading, just as he
had hoped and planned. Men were starting to recognize
him on sight.

He also saw the sheriff sitting in front of his office. He
was sure the man had also recognized him, even though
he gave no outward sign of having done so. Nevertheless,
he touched his hand to the brim of his hat as he passed,
a friendly, respectful gesture to the local law.

Garrett, he thought, Wild Bull Hanson has arrived.

Clint and Bonney remained where they were, waiting
to see if Hanson would choose this hotel. There was one
other in town, but this one was the nearest to the livery.
Sure enough, the man came walking back toward them,
carrying his saddlebags and rifle. Just as Clint had com-

mented, Hanson did not walk so much as strut. He looked idiotic to Clint as he approached the hotel.

As Hanson got nearer, Bonney could not help but stare. He had never seen Wild Bill Hickok and so did not know how closely Hanson had made himself resemble the famous gunman. His mustache and beard were carefully trimmed, his hair was long and curled up on the shoulders of his buckskin jacket.

As Hanson went by them he looked at them both very pointedly, as if daring them to say or do something. Bonney looked away, but Clint did not.

As Hanson passed from view and entered the hotel, Clint found himself disliking the man even more than he thought he would.

FORTY-TWO

"He's . . . formidable-looking," Bonney said.

"He looks like a clown."

"But his eyes—"

"False confidence."

"What do you mean?"

"He didn't have anything to fear from us—or so he thought."

"But he does?"

"If you're smart, you realize that anyone can be a danger to you, no matter how harmless they appear."

"You don't appear harmless."

"You do."

Bonney accepted that in stride.

"What do we do now?"

"We wait."

"Why?" Bonney asked. "Why don't we talk to him now?"

"Well, for one thing," Clint said, "the sheriff has been watching us."

Bonney looked around, then finally located the lawman sitting in front of his office.

"How long?" he asked.

"Since yesterday."

"Why didn't you tell me?"

"I didn't want you to do what you just did."

"Wha—"

"You looked over there."

Bonney quickly turned his eyes toward the ground and said, "Oh."

"Come on."

"Where?"

"The saloon."

Bonney frowned.

"The monotony, remember?" Clint said.

And Bonney did remember. Put your horse in the livery, check into your hotel, and go to the nearest saloon.

Sheriff Starr watched as the first two strangers walked to the saloon and entered. Soon, he knew, the third one would also walk over there. No real trouble yet, so he decided to keep waiting.

When Bull Hanson came out of the hotel he looked at the two empty chairs. The younger man, the one who had looked away, would not be a problem, but the other one . . . well, that might be a different story. Still, once they knew for sure who he was, he was sure there wouldn't be a problem.

He stepped off the boardwalk and crossed the street to go to the nearest saloon.

•   •   •

As Hanson entered the saloon the sheriff got up to go back into his office. He stopped abruptly when he saw the three men riding down the street. More strangers, and these three hard cases, from the looks of them. They also looked enough alike to be brothers.

He watched as they rode by and didn't even look his way. Now there were six strangers in town, and when was the last time that had happened?

Never.

Starr was nervous now. For a man who didn't like confrontations, six strangers in town at one time was a little much to bear.

He decided to go into his office and stay there until he figured out how to handle the situation.

FORTY-THREE

As Hanson entered the saloon, Clint and Bonney saw him from a back table.

"This should be interesting," Bonney said.

"What should?"

"Well, he's going to want to sit with his back to the wall, isn't he?"

"Probably."

"There aren't any of those tables available."

"There's always somebody who's easily intimidated," Clint said.

"You mean—"

"Watch," Clint said. "If this man is the phony I think he is . . . well, just watch."

Hanson went to the bar, got himself a beer, then turned and looked around the saloon. To Clint's practiced eye his movements were mannered, as if he were onstage, playing the part of the dangerous, ominous stranger.

Finally, Hanson's eyes fell on his victim. He approached a man seated at a table alone, about two tables away from where Clint and Bonney were seated. Hanson stopped in front of the table and stared down at the man. The man looked back up at him for a few moments, then swallowed, got up, and not only left the table, but the saloon, as well.

"But . . . he didn't say a word," Bonney said.

"He didn't have to," Clint said. "I'll give him this, he knows how to pick them."

"Pick who?"

"The people who will buy into his playacting."

"Playacting?"

"He's a phony, D. L."

"I thought you had to talk to him to find that out."

"No," Clint said, "I just have to watch him."

"Well . . . when are we going to talk to him?"

Clint thought a moment, then said, "Now."

"Can I come along?"

"Sure."

Clint stood up and walked to Hanson's table, with Bonney right behind him. The younger man was surprised when Clint just walked up to the other man's table and sat down without saying a word. Hesitantly, he took another chair, sitting right on the edge.

Hanson gave them both a long look, then put his beer mug down and narrowed his eyes. Clint assumed that the narrowing of the eyes was supposed to scare him.

"I don't remember invitin' you gents to set down." That's what he said, "set" down. Clint thought that the accent he was using was as phony as the rest of him. The only real thing about the man was his guns. They were decent Colts, well cared for. Give him credit for that, then.

"You're Hanson, aren't you?" Clint asked.

"That's right, stranger," Hanson said. "You recognized me, huh?"

"No," Clint said, "not you, just the ludicrous getup."

Bonney caught his breath.

"What did you say?" Hanson asked, staring hard at Clint, who seemed completely relaxed.

"I said you look ludicrous," Clint repeated. "Do you know what that means?"

"Well—"

"Tell him, D. L."

"Uh . . ." Bonney said.

"Go ahead," Clint said, "tell him what it means."

"Well . . . it, uh, means . . . silly."

"I know what it means, sonny," Hanson said. He could call Bonney "sonny" because he was at least ten years older. "Are you sayin' I look silly?" he demanded of Clint.

"I'm sorry," Clint said. "Didn't I speak English? You . . . look . . . ridiculous!"

Clint said it loud enough to draw the attention of everyone in the room.

"Do you know who you're talkin' to?" Hanson asked.

"I'm talking to a silly ass who thinks he's a Hickok look-alike."

"Mister," Hanson said, "you better think real hard—"

Clint cut him off again.

"Let me introduce you to this man, Hanson," Clint said. "His name is D. L. Bonney. He's a writer from back East. He came here to write about you."

Hanson looked at Bonney with renewed interest.

"Really?"

"That's right," Clint said. "He seems to think you're some kind of legend of the West."

"Word's got to the East, huh?" Hanson asked with a satisfied look.

"Oh, it got there, all right," Clint said, "just like you planned. But word is also going to get to the East that you're a phony."

Hanson's look turned hard again, but to Clint it was hardly a deterrent.

"What'd you say?"

"I said you're a phony," Clint said. "You gave yourself the name *Wild* Bull, and you spread some stories around that some people believed, and you think you're a legend."

"Mister, I don't know who you are," Hanson said, "but you're about a hair away from—"

"Adams."

"What?"

"My name's Adams," Clint said. "Clint Adams."

Hanson stared at him, and Clint waited. Bonney watched Hanson's face as it started to crumple, first around the eyes and then the smugly set mouth. The man's face grew red, then pale, and he licked his lips.

"Adams . . ." he said in a low voice.

"That's right."

"The, uh . . . Gunsmith?"

"That's him," Bonney said, suddenly finding his voice.

All of the energy seemed to leave Hanson's body. His shoulders slumped, his arms went limp, and he seemed to shrink in his chair.

"I don't know how long you thought you were going to get away with it, Hanson," Clint said, "but the game's over."

Bonney was amazed at the change in Hanson's demeanor. Once again Clint Adams had read someone entirely correctly.

"Wasn't doin' no harm," Hanson muttered.

"The only harm you were going to do was to yourself," Clint said. "Eventually you would have gotten yourself killed."

"I—"

"How many men have you killed, Mr. Hanson?" Bonney asked.

Hanson looked at Bonney and then away.

"We heard that the total was somewhere over twenty."

"Twenty-two, wasn't it?" Clint asked. "You kill that many men, Mr. Hanson?"

"Well . . ." Hanson said, "no . . ."

"How many?" Clint asked. "How many, then?"

Clint was surprised that he wasn't enjoying this more. He hadn't expected the man to cave in so easily.

"I . . . I ain't ever killed nobody."

"Why doesn't that surprise me?" Clint asked. "What the hell were you thinking, man? You think this kind of a reputation is something to play with?"

"I've seen the way people step out of the way when a man with a reputation walks their way," Hanson said. "Nobody ever treated me with that much respect . . . or fear."

"So you decided to do some playacting?"

"That's what I am," Hanson said.

"What are you talking about?" Clint asked.

"I'm an actor," Hanson said, "at least, I was, but I wasn't very good at that either. I thought if I could convince people that I was a deadly shot, a dangerous man, I could prove that I was a good actor."

Clint stared at Hanson in amazement, but it was Bonney who spoke.

"You what?" He stood up.

Suddenly, Hanson was looking at Bonney in fear.

"I came all this way to . . . to . . . write about an actor?"

It was the angriest Clint had ever seen D. L. Bonney.

"D. L., take it easy."

"No!" Bonney said. "This . . . phony made me waste
. . . weeks of my life!"

"Think about it," Clint said, putting his hand on Bonney's arm. "How many other things did you find to write
about?"

Bonney glared at him for a moment, then relented.

"A lot."

"You bet, a lot," Clint said. "He did you a favor
bringing you out here. Now sit down."

Bonney hesitated just a moment, then sat down.

"Thanks," Hanson said.

"Don't thank me," Clint said. "You still have me to
deal with."

"Whataya mean?"

Before Clint could answer a man came walking into the
saloon, looked around, and then walked to their table. He
looked past Clint and Bonney right at Hanson.

"Are you Wild Bull Hanson?"

Hanson looked at Clint, as if seeking the proper answer.

"He is," Bonney said.

"Well," the man said, glancing at Bonney then looking
back at Hanson, "there are three men outside who say
their name is Tappia."

"What?" Hanson asked, confused.

"Tappia," the man said again. "They say you killed
their brother, and they're waiting outside for you."

"What?" Hanson said again.

"There are three men outside waiting to kill you,"
Bonney said with great satisfaction. "That is, unless you
kill them first."

FORTY-FOUR

"You gotta help me."

"Why?" Clint asked.

"If I go out there they'll kill me."

"Did you start the rumor that you shot their brother?" Bonney asked.

"I don't even know who their brother is."

"Bobby Tappia," Bonney said. "Does the name ring a bell?"

Hanson looked panicked.

"I . . . claimed credit for killing a lot of men," he said. "I don't remember their names. I'd just . . . hear about them being killed and start saying I did it."

"And you never thought it would come to this?" Clint asked.

"I . . . didn't think about it."

"Well, think about it now," Bonney said, "because they're waiting for you."

"Adams," Hanson said, "you gotta help me."

"Why?" Clint asked again.

"They'll never stand up to you," Hanson said. "You can back them down."

"Why should I?"

"They'll kill me."

"Whose fault is that?"

"This isn't funny!"

"I don't think any of this is funny, Hanson," Clint said. "For one thing you're defaming the name of a good friend of mine."

"What?"

"Why did you decide to dress up as Wild Bill Hickok?" Clint asked.

"I . . ." Hanson shrugged. "He was the only one I knew, that I could copy. Look." He took off his hat, and then his hair. "See? It's a wig."

"Jesus," Bonney said. "What about the beard and mustache?"

Hanson touched them.

"I was able to grow them myself."

He put the hat and hair on the table and looked imploringly at Clint.

"You gotta help me."

At that moment a man entered the saloon. Clint recognized him as the sheriff.

"Over here, Sheriff," he called.

The man frowned and walked over.

"My name's Clint Adams."

"The Gunsmith?"

"That's right," Bonney said, "and this is Wild Bull Hanson."

The sheriff looked at Hanson and registered surprise.

"What happened to your hair?"

"It's not my hair," Hanson said, "it's a wig—and my

name's not Wild Bull Hanson, it's just plain Eddie Hanson.''

"What?"

"He's not a gunfighter," Bonney said, "he's an actor." He looked at Clint. "You know, this won't make a bad story."

"An actor?" the sheriff said. "I've got three men out in the street waiting to gun down an actor?"

"I guess so," Bonney said.

"No!" Hanson said, burying his face in his hands.

"If I go out there and tell them this," the sheriff said, "they're not gonna believe it. They'll shoot up my town."

"You're the law," Hanson said. "You gotta stop them."

"Son," the sheriff said, "I've been the law here for twelve years. Do you know how I lasted this long?"

"How?" Bonney asked with interest.

"Never bit off more than I could chew."

"Huh?" Bonney said.

"By *not* going out into the street to face three gunmen."

"Well, if he doesn't do it," Bonney said, "and Hanson doesn't do it . . ."

"Right," Clint said, aware that everyone was looking at him.

"Hanson!" a voice called from the street. "Bull Hanson! If you're not out here in three minutes we're gonna start shooting up the town."

"Oh, God . . ." Hanson said.

"Relax, Hanson," Clint said. "I'll take care of it."

Clint stopped just inside the batwing doors and saw three men standing in the street, spread out. He knew immediately that, unlike the men in Weatherby, these three knew what they were doing.

There were a couple of ways he could do this. One, he could try to talk them out of it. Two, he could draw and kill them. If the sheriff of Zackel was right, and one of them killed that whore, he'd be bringing the killer to justice—but what about the other two men? If they knew about the killing, then they were accessories.

He was going to have to let the three Tappia brothers make the decision on their own.

"D. L.?"

"Yes?"

"Bring me the hat," Clint said, "and the hair."

"What? What for?"

"Just bring it."

Bonney grabbed the hat and wig from the table and brought them to Clint.

"Hanson?"

"Yes, sir?" Very respectful now.

"Bring me your guns."

Hanson rose slowly, took the gun belt off, and brought it to Clint.

"What are you going to do?"

"They want Wild Bull Hanson," Clint said, "I'm going to give you to them."

"Wha—"

"Just go and sit down."

Hanson went back to the table.

"Sheriff?"

"Yeah?"

"Are you coming out with me?"

"I'm afraid not, Adams," the lawman said. "You're on your own."

"Why doesn't that surprise me?"

He stepped outside.

FORTY-FIVE

Clint stepped out of the saloon and onto the walk. The three men stiffened, but nobody went for their gun—not yet.

"Who are you?" one of them asked. "You're not Hanson."

This was the older one talking.

"You must be Jimmy Tappia."

"How do you know who I am?"

"I know who you all are, Tappia. I also know one of you killed a woman in Zackel."

Jimmy Tappia was standing between his brothers, who each tossed him an anxious look.

"Look, friend, I don't know who you are—"

"My name is Clint Adams, Tappia."

"Adams?"

"T-that's the Gunsmith," one of the others said.

"Quiet, Jesse!"

"You're looking for Wild Bull Hanson, right?"

"He killed our brother Bobby," Jimmy Tappia said, "and now we're gonna kill him."

Clint had the hat, wig, and gun belt in his left hand. Now he threw them all into the street. The three brothers jumped, as if he'd tossed snakes at their feet, but no one went for his gun.

"What the hell is that?" Jimmy Tappia demanded.

"That's Bull Hanson," Clint said. "That's all he ever was. A hat and some guns."

"What do you mean?"

"I mean there is no Bull Hanson, Tappia," Clint said. "He never existed, and he never killed your brother."

"You're crazy."

"It was a hoax, Tappia," Clint said. "The whole Wild Bull Hanson personality was an act, the reputation a pack of lies."

"What are you saying?"

"I'm telling you you'll have to look for your brother's killer somewhere else. There is no Wild Bull Hanson."

"You're a liar."

"Jimmy—" one of the brothers said.

"Shut up!"

"Jimmy! He's the Gunsmith."

"There's three of us!"

"Listen to your brother, Jimmy," Clint said. "You have to be alive to avenge your brother's death."

"Goddamn you—" Jimmy Tappia said and went for his gun.

Clint normally made a killing shot when he drew, but he had more time here than usual. Jimmy Tappia was no gunquick, and Clint instinctively knew that his brothers would not back his play.

He drew and fired. His slung struck Tappia in the right

shoulder, deadening his arm. Jimmy never got his gun out of the holster.

"How about you, boys?" Clint asked.

"No, no," one of the brothers said, throwing his hands in the air.

"Don't shoot," the one called Jesse said.

Jimmy Tappia had sunk to his knees, left hand pressed to his right shoulder.

"Take your brother away, boys," Clint said.

"What you said about Hanson, is that true?" one of them asked.

"It's true," Clint said. "He was just a liar, an actor playing a role."

"T-then where do we look for our brother's killer?"

Clint shrugged.

"That's your problem. I'll tell you this, though. One of you killed a woman in Zackel. You're going to have to pay for that."

"I-it was an accident," Jesse Tappia said.

"That's your problem, too, boys," Clint said. "Take your brother and go back home. That's the best piece of advice I can give you."

The two brothers nodded and helped their older brother to his feet. As they helped him walk away, the sheriff came out of the saloon.

"One shot," he said, "that wasn't bad."

Clint holstered his gun and looked at the man.

"You're not much of a lawman, are you, Sheriff?"

The man shrugged.

"I'm still alive," he said. "That's what counts."

The sheriff stepped into the street and walked away. Clint couldn't argue with his logic.

D. L. Bonney and Eddie Hanson came out next. In the street lay the hat, wig, and guns.

"That's what's left of Wild Bull Hanson, Eddie," Clint

said. "I think you better stick to being yourself from now on."

"I think you're right, Mr. Adams."

"Eddie?" Bonney said. "Can we talk?"

"About what?"

"About what drives a man to do what you did."

"Found something to write about, D. L.?" Clint asked.

"I found a lot to write about, Clint," Bonney said, "but I think I'll start right here."

Clint nodded and said, "That's probably a good start."

Watch for

THE QUEENSVILLE TEMPTRESS

179th novel in the exciting GUNSMITH series
from Jove

Coming in November!

J. R. ROBERTS

THE
GUNSMITH